Hero Unleashed

Anna Alexander

Hero Unleashed

Anna Alexander

Book two in the Heroes of Saturn series.

Princess Amaryllis should have been sad to be exiled from her home on the Saturn moon, but on Earth she finds freedoms she never imagined existed. She embraces her new home with big, open-mouthed kisses and establishes herself as a prominent businesswoman catering to the humans' most intimate desires. When the former head of her father's guard enters her domain, he rouses not only old insecurities but also a burning desire to see him lose the formal constraints and succumb to the promise in his command.

Lucian Kilsgaard was a warrior without a mission until he received word that an assassin had been sent to ensure the exiled princess does not return to reclaim the throne. He goes to warn the princess and instead of the unconfident, impulsive girl he remembers, he finds a bold temptress. How can he protect her when all he wants is to sink into her softness? He vows the line between protector and lover will never be crossed, yet Amaryllis will test his resolve until he takes exactly what he needs.

Dedication

To my MOTHER and Lana. Yes, you will have to share. And as always, to my chicklets.

Find Anna Online

Website

annaalexander.net

Facebook

facebook.com/pages/Anna-Alexander/282170065189471

Twitter

twitter.com/AnnaWriter

Newsletter

http://eepurl.com/Q0tsz

Chapter One

"**W**HAT IS THAT?**" Lucian asked, pointing to a red star growing larger in the night sky.

"I was wondering the same thing about that one right there." His brother Kristos gestured to a spot over their heads.

The star burned a brilliant blue with a gold light trailing behind it like stardust. More streaks of white and silver blazed across the blue-black background in the largest meteor shower to blaze over Washington state in twenty years. The sight really was spectacular, but Lucian's interest was firmly focused on the two orbs and their vivid colors that pulsated like warning beacons.

Kristos rose from where he had been reclining on the grass with his wife, Brett. She too jumped to her feet and grabbed his hand. "Kristos, what is it? You two sense something."

"I don't know, *alskata*."

"You know, boys," "Uncle" Harlan said as he joined Lucian at the edge of the deck, "that looks a lot like your spacecraft did when you crashed to Earth."

Lucian froze as his heart rate doubled. He didn't need to look at his brother to know they shared the same thought, for his empathetic powers picked up Kristos' excitement and trepidation like a punch in the sternum.

They all held their breath as the closest sphere appeared to slow its trajectory and the blue light flickered like a flame going out.

"It's heading for the gulch." Brett reached for her boots and tugged them on. "The red one is too far away to tell where it'll end up."

The blue ball disappeared into the tree line about a mile from their location. A second later the ground trembled beneath their feet as a plume of light shot into the air.

"I'll don the armor," Kristos called out, barely beating Lucian to the back door as they raced into the house with Brett hot on their heels.

Lucian dashed to his room. From under his bed he withdrew his short sword and scabbard. He buckled it around his hips as he bolted back into the hall. It wasn't necessary for both he and his brother to don the royal armor. Besides, he was too impatient to change his clothes.

"Lucian, wait for me." Brett pulled on her coat, marking her as sheriff, and tightened her own belt loaded with her pistol and Taser.

"Brett, you're not going," Kristos shouted from his former room.

She paid him no heed. "Who knows how many others saw that explosion? I'll do my best to keep people from investigating."

On this, Lucian agreed. Kristos could fight, and lose again, the ongoing battle over Brett's profession another day.

Harlan met them outside. He checked the barrel of a shotgun before setting it in the front seat of his truck. "I'll meet you out there."

"Yes sir." Lucian crouched down low. "Climb on my back, sister. We'll be faster on foot. Ready?"

"Yep."

Brett was a light weight to carry on his back, her knees locked onto his sides and one arm banded across his chest as he ran with speed and grace into the night. With her other hand she grasped her police radio. "Unit one to base. Come in please."

"This is base. Sheriff, we're having a lot of calls coming in about an explosion out in the gulch."

"I'm already at the scene. It appears that the good people of Cedar got a little more up close and personal with the meteor shower tonight. It's nothing major, just a good-size chunk of rock and a nose full of dust. There aren't any flames, so let the captain know that a crew isn't necessary. I'll do some more investigating, and if something sparks, I'll call him in."

"10-4, Sheriff."

She shoved the radio onto her belt. "There won't be any flames, right?"

"How would I know? I was inside the module when we crashed. That's a better question for Harlan."

"Jiminy Christmas," she muttered and clung on tighter. "I've bought us maybe five minutes. Someone's bound to be suspicious and come calling."

"We'll be there in one."

Brett let out a startled shriek and tested the integrity of his shirt with her clutching fingers as he blazed a trail through the brush and bramble of the forest. His two hearts beat hard and fast, not from exertion, but with an excitement he hadn't experienced since long before he and Kristos had been banished from their home planet.

Deep in his gut, Lucian knew that whatever it was that crashed to Earth was not a simple meteor and the urge to laugh tightened his throat. Where was his usual vigilance to remain aloof and avoid entanglements with humankind? He was usually the one to caution his impetuous brother to hide their abilities and to forget that they were once great warriors and live the life of unassuming, law-abiding citizens.

Oh but now. Now the flush of impending action fired his muscles, driving him forward to face the unknown. To search for the treasure he didn't think he ever wanted again.

A purpose.

Lucian set Brett on her feet as they approached the smoldering wreckage. His lips tightened against a shout of anticipation inspired by the sight of the oval-shaped pod nestled in the dirt. The cobalt-blue paint was scraped to the bare metal and the once-smooth sides were crumpled, looking as if the whole thing had been brushed with coarse sandpaper.

Brett let loose with a low whistle and swept her hand toward the fallen trees and scorched bushes around them. "Holy shit. Look at this destruction. That trail has to be at least a few hundred yards. People are going to expect a gigantic meteor caused all this."

"We'll cover the tracks," Lucian replied absentmindedly. His attention was fixed firmly on the craft before them.

He reached out a hand and snapped it back from the too-hot metal. Eager to know who was inside, he circled around the perimeter in search of clues.

The crunch of leaves signaled Kristos' arrival. He wore the Skandavian royal uniform, including the black cowl that covered most of his face. A tunic of finely woven minerals clung to his chest and back. The material protected the wearer from a slice from a sword or a hit from a blast gun, and also refracted light so it blended in with the surroundings. In the dark, Kristos was nearly invisible.

"By the Gods," he exclaimed. "It is one of ours."

"Any idea who it may be?" Brett asked.

Lucian gestured to the faint symbol etched in the metal. "This insignia marks it as a royal."

"The King?" Kristos gasped. "I don't believe it. And if it is, he can kiss my ass."

Lucian shared a similar sentiment, however he wouldn't have phrased it in such a manner. "Help me roll it right-side up. Watch out. It's still hot."

Together they maneuvered the pod to a position that gave them access to the seam where the two halves met. This was an escape pod, only to be used in times of emergency. If the palace were to come under attack and the guard had fallen, one or two people could use the craft and escape to one of the neighboring moons. Traveling to somewhere as distant as Earth was suicidal in such a vehicle. That honor was reserved solely for banishment. And Lucian and his brother were the first to have received that honor.

"Perhaps it's your missing princess," Brett suggested. "She's the only other royal left, right?"

"No." Kristos immediately rejected the idea. "She disappeared long before we were sent away. How do we get this open?"

"I hear Harlan coming now." Lucian ran to meet the truck where it parked at the top of the rise. "It's one of ours. Did you bring any of your tools?"

"They're in the back." Harlan opened the tailgate and reached for a battered toolbox. He withdrew a crowbar and a large rubber mallet. "Here. This is what I used to spring you boys free."

"Thank you." He rushed back down the hill. "Stand back."

He wedged the flat end of the crowbar against the seam. Despite the damage to the hull, there was very little room to slip in the tool. With his super strength it took only three blows of the hammer to bust the seal. The top gave way with a hiss and popped open a few inches. He lifted the hatch and peered into the dimly lit interior.

A few lights flickered, sputtering out one by one with the loss of pressure. A green glow remained around the figure slumped in the forward seat. By the breadth of the shoulders, Lucian guessed it to be male. His face was covered by a mask that fed the wearer breathable air, and kept the lungs from being crushed during entry. With the man being unconscious, there were no emotions to give away the motive for the trip or a hint of identity. The man was attired in the same manner as Kristos. His uniform declaring him a fellow guard.

"Shine a light this way," Lucian ordered and jumped into the pod, squeezing his big body between the console and seat.

He turned the valves on the mask to carefully adjust the mixture of air and slowly acclimate the stranger to the new environment. The air on Earth was thinner than on Skandavia but very similar. Still, too much at once gave you such a headache, you wished you hadn't made it through entry. When it was safe to shut off the valve, Lucian unlatched the headgear and removed the mask.

"Great Being," he whispered. "Dhavin."

Lucian pulled back the cowl and laid his palms on the man's cheeks and wrapped his fingers around the base of his skull, measuring the temperature and clamminess of the skin. He pried open Dhavin's eyelids and watched as the pupils dilated and constricted in an attempt to focus. At the base of his neck the pulse was weak but steady. A harness had kept Dhavin firmly in his seat, but from experience Lucian knew that beneath the straps deep bruises were already forming. Other than the obvious, Dhavin looked for the most part unharmed.

"Do you know him?" Brett asked, with Taser in hand.

"It's our cousin," Kristos answered as Lucian worked on releasing the harness.

"Come on, Dhavin. Wake up." He shook his younger cousin's shoulders and tapped him on the cheek. "Wake up. Show me you made it through."

Dark lashes fluttered ever so slightly as a crease formed on his forehead. Lucian held his breath as he watched consciousness slowly return and Dhavin struggle to open his eyes. After several tries, the lids finally lifted. He looked up and gasped when he spotted Lucian.

"I found you." The words came out on a sigh. Tears filled his brown eyes as his face crumpled. "I found you."

"You most certainly did." He kept a bracing hand on his cousin and reached out with his emotions for any sign of pain. "Not that I'm unhappy to see you, but what in icy hells are you doing here?"

Dhavin jolted at the words. It took a considerable amount of strength to lift his hand and place it over Lucian's, managing a firm squeeze of importance. "Warn you. King's dead. Assassin. After you. Kristos."

"After us? Why?"

"You—" He began to pant and his eyes rolled back. "You. Know."

"Know what?" He barely managed to keep his tone level. He grasped Dhavin by the arms and shook. "Know what?"

His head flopped back as he whispered, "The princess."

"Amaryllis?" he breathed in surprise then winced.

Never should he think of the princess so informally, yet after all this time, he had begun to think of her as belonging solely to him. Only in his fantasies did he address her in such a manner, which he only allowed because he couldn't fault his subconscious. But he'd best remember to mind his place in the future. His beautiful, delicate princess was in danger and as her guard, he needed to be focused on her protection.

"Dhavin. Dhavin!" He shook his cousin by the shoulders with barely leashed restraint. With every passing second, his princess could be lost. Answers were required. Now.

"Ah!" Dhavin's eyes snapped open and he grimaced. "What is happening to me? By the Gods, I feel like *rohaul* dung."

At this, Lucian smiled a mere fraction. "You'll never believe me. Just wait. You're still adjusting to the climate. It will wear off and then you'll be up doing things you've never dreamed."

"Like lift my head?"

"And so much more. Come on, we need to get you indoors."

Dhavin started as Kristos reached out a hand to assist him from the craft. "Kristos, is that you?"

"Ya. It's good to see you, cousin. I'm going to have my wife Brett and another friend of ours help you to the conveyance. You've made quite an entrance we need to conceal."

"Wife? You found a woman who would have you?"

"She couldn't resist my charm."

"Charm?" Brett asked as she slipped under Dhavin's arm. "I would have called it begging and pleading."

Lucian left Harlan and Brett to help Dhavin up the incline to the truck and went to tackle the wrecked spaceship. From inside a compartment under the seat, he pulled out a small gel-filled explosive and attached the grenade to the waistband of his jeans. In minutes the Earth's nitrogen-rich atmosphere would break down the combustible components, rendering the bomb useless, but he only required a little of the accelerant to suit his purpose.

"Kristos. Grab the other end. On two," he commanded when they settled into place.

Together they easily managed to get the craft onto the flatbed. Kristos used his super speed to create a whirlwind that destroyed the majority of the path of torn shrubs and fallen trees, ripping trunks out of the ground to make it look as if they had never been there in the first place. Lucian retrieved a pony-sized boulder from along the bank of the nearby Cedar River. Breaking the seal on the grenade, he doused the boulder with the gel and reattached the empty shell to his belt.

"Incoming," he warned, then lifted the boulder above his head and let it fly.

The stone soared high in the air before retracing the ship's original landing path and settling into the vacant hole. It wasn't a perfect cover, but it would do.

"Boys, company's on the way," Brett shouted. "Call just

came over the radio. Reutgers pulled a van over for speeding three miles from here. The occupants stated they were heading toward the meteor."

"We're done here." Lucian jumped onto the flatbed next to Kristos and thumped the top of the cab where the others were squashed inside. "Don't bother taking it easy, Harlan. Time is of the essence."

"Watch the ruts." Lucian heard Brett caution. "We don't know what injuries he has."

"He can take it. He's a *Llanos*."

The look she shot him through the back window relayed exactly how she felt about that statement.

Despite Brett's sentiments, Harlan took the most direct, which also meant the bumpiest, route back to the house. Once they were safely ensconced in the garage, they all piled out.

"I appreciate the concern, little cousin," Dhavin chided with a smile in his voice as Brett took his arm and lead him into the living room. "But I need to walk on my own. You don't show weakness in front of the general."

"That was back on Skandavia. Around here, I'm in charge. You've just experienced a major trauma and need to rest. You can lie down in Kristos' old room."

"This lounge will do fine." Dhavin all but melted over the couch's leather upholstery. His exhaustion and pain belied his easy smile, but Lucian sensed the difficulty it took him to simply draw a breath.

"Do you think your stomach can handle anything to eat?

What can I bring him?" she asked.

"Tea and some bread will be fine to start," Lucian answered.

"I'll be right back. And don't bother talking in another language. I will find out what's going on."

Dhavin watched her leave with an admiring gleam in his eyes. "By the Gods, Kristos. Her coloring matches yours. You didn't just bond, you mated. Congratulations. Leave it to you to make a haven from what was to be a punishment."

"Thank you." Kristos pulled at a blond lock of his hair. When he bonded with his mate, the black strands changed to match her honey tresses and her eyes had gone from hazel to equal his jade in the mating tradition of their people. "We're still finding our rhythm, but even our worst days are among the happiest of my life."

"She's beautiful. Very strong of heart."

"That she is. And if you think one inappropriate thought about her, I'll break every bone in your body."

His rusty chuckle turned into a cough that nearly bent him in two. "Gah, I hate this weakness."

"It will pass." Lucian sat on a nearby chair, eager to bypass the pleasantries of reuniting. "Dhavin, what happened? You said the king was dead."

"Ya. Not long after you were sent away, the king began to lose his command over the guard. Many were loyal to you and Kristos, even though they would never admit it out loud."

"They shouldn't have been," Kristos said. "It was my fault

the queen was killed."

"We all knew you would have given your life for hers. You did your best. That is why we remained loyal. Stavos was picked as your replacement, Lucian, but he didn't have your knowledge or the heart. It was too easy for Hamerkind to regroup his men and defeat the throne. The king was executed, as well as a good number of the guard, including Stavos."

"I'm sorry for your loss, Dhavin. Your brother was a good man."

He closed his eyes and took several long breaths then whispered, "Nothing was the same after you left."

His grief reached out and squeezed Lucian around the heart. Desperation for more information tightened his throat, but as much as he wanted to interrogate his cousin, he knew the man had to tell his story at his own pace.

"The rest of the men in my ring and myself took to the tunnels, gathering information and rebuilding the guard. Hamerkind has the throne, but he does not have the people. The lords were dissatisfied with the king, but they don't want Hamerkind. Since he is not royal, they aren't complying with his wishes, and he doesn't have the manpower to implore a dictatorship...yet. There is talk that if the princess returns, the Hall of Lords will recognize her authority and Hamerkind loses his power. Especially with you as her guard."

"And how were we to return?" Kristos snorted. "They sent us away in a craft clearly meant for one flight, without any forms of communication. The only reason we had our weapons is because Stavos hid them in the pod before we launched."

"Please, your brother is the great General Lucianllanos. It was only his honor that got him banished. If anyone could find a way to return, it is Lucian."

Kristos choked on a laugh as Lucian straightened in his seat and inclined his head. "Thank you for the compliment, but it is practically impossible to return. I've tested the possibility."

"Practically. That is not a for certain, and this Hamerkind knows, which is why he sent the assassin."

"Who?"

"Bale."

"Impossible," Kristos scoffed. "Bale would never accept such a mission from Hamerkind."

"Yes, he would." Lucian stood and paced the few steps from the chair to the window. "He blames me for what happened to his wife and child."

"You had nothing to do with that attack on their colony."

"No, not directly, but we knew they were one of the potential targets and I forbade him from going to their defense."

"Bale would have died with them if he had gone."

Lucian looked his brother in the eye. "He died with them anyway."

All of the *Llanos* had died a bit when they discovered the smoldering carnage that had once been a thriving farming community. Agriculture was a highly prized industry that the little colony had excelled in, which also made them a prime target for Hamerkind to use against the king. No man, woman or child survived the decimation.

After he buried his family, Bale had gone on a rampage and singlehandedly took out the entire platoon who had destroyed his colony. The quiet, steadfast man Lucian had relied on in the thick of battle had been replaced by a cauldron of hate that boiled so hotly, it burned everything in its path. Consumed with rage, Bale left the guard, but not before he attempted to take Lucian's life. He had the passion, but Lucian had the skill and was able to defeat the attack. Barely. He was a threat Lucian would never underestimate.

"So Bale gets his revenge by killing you. But what does he get out of murdering the princess?" Kristos asked.

"Anything he wants." Dhavin chuckled mirthlessly. "All he has to do is return with your heads and Hamerkind will give him whatever he desires."

"That's all well and good, but he'll have to defeat us first."

"Careful, Kristos," Lucian warned. "We have to assume that Bale will receive the same powers as we did. He'll be a danger to us and anyone else he comes into contact with. We have to be prepared."

Dhavin struggled to sit up. "And the princess. She must be warned."

"Good luck with that," said Kristos. "Have any idea where she disappeared to?"

His eyes widened with surprise as he looked toward Lucian. "You didn't tell him?"

"Tell me what?" Kristos shot his brother a frown.

Lucian narrowed his gaze at his cousin. "What would you know, Dhavin?"

"Are you serious? I was her guard, and her friend, like I wouldn't suspect. Why didn't you tell Kristos?"

"Tell me what? Lucian?" Kristos got in his face, his bright eyes blazed a brilliant green. "What are you keeping from me?"

He lifted his chin and confessed, "The princess is here, in the city."

Chapter Two

H IS ERECTION WAS impressive, but it was obvious he had no idea how to use it.

Amaryllis turned away from her dance partner and bit back a smile when he pulled her against his wildly gyrating hips. Her handsome Latino was a sexy thing, but he danced as if his pants were on fire. Alejandro was so eager to please she didn't have the heart to bruise his ego and damage the confidence she sensed it took him to gather to ask her to dance. She took his hands to guide his arms around her waist and swung her hips in a slow sway. He quickly fell into her rhythm, cuddling her close enough to brush his lips along her bare shoulder and bathe her skin with a soft sigh. Hmm, perhaps he could be trained.

She took her own deep breath and soaked in the energy of the bodies writhing on the dance floor. The Cavern was her personal playground, created to celebrate life. A place that accepted all types, no matter race, shape or orientation, and the only thing that turned you away from the door was a piss-poor attitude. It was a paradise created out of mahogany and leather.

Sex and adrenaline rode along the air in waves that vibrated like the booming bass from the nearby speakers. Within these walls fears were being faced, taboos broken and the limits of the human body pushed to the extremes. Above the dance floor acrobats swung from trapezes and showered the dancers in bursts of confetti, ratcheting up the mayhem. With her empathic abilities, Amaryllis siphoned myriad emotions, maintaining a high of arousal and excitement greater than any drug in the known universe. These were her people. This was living.

"May I touch you, please?" her potential lover murmured in her ear, tightening the hold around her waist.

That he asked permission pleased her. Yes, he most certainly was a candidate to be trained.

"Where do you want to touch me?"

"Everywhere." He chuckled and nipped at her neck. "Right now, your breasts."

She smiled in response and settled in his embrace. "You may touch me. Go slow."

He raked his fingernails up over the silk covering her torso and back down her belly. Up and down. Up and down. Each stroke brought his palms closer to the mounds that grew heavy with anticipation.

Just as quick as a candle being snuffed out, her arousal was quenched. To those who continued to dance, nothing appeared amiss, but a disturbance ripped through the air that made her nipples tighten even as the hair on her arms stood on end.

"Let her go," came the gruff command.

The authority in his tone plucked the strings of a forgotten memory. Where did she know that voice?

"She's fine with me," her dance partner protested.

"You will leave her now."

A cool breeze hit her back a second later, as she was suddenly left on her own to face the interloper.

Hmm, perhaps he was a bit too submissive.

Amaryllis straightened her shoulders and turned to politely tell the dance-crasher to fuck off, only to rock back on her heels. She didn't think her tongue fell out of her mouth but her eyes definitely boggled as she looked her fill. The Gods did well when they created this impressive male specimen.

"Lucianllanos," she whispered, trapped in a vortex of past and present.

She had forgotten how tall the head of the guard was, how broad his shoulders and how massive the muscles that stretched his long-sleeved chambray shirt. Black wavy hair fell to his shoulders and framed his strong jaw and high cheekbones. But his eyes… Oh now his green gaze was just as fierce as she remembered.

In her former life Lucian was what she'd label as "other". He had been her father's personal guard as well as commander of all *Llanos*, so she never allowed herself permission to give the general much thought, aside from the appreciation a woman felt when looking at an attractive, virile man. But as he stood before her now, that admiration was escalating into a rolling boil of awareness that made perspiration gather along her hairline.

The don't-fuck-with-me vibe he wore was so effective, the crowd of dancers gave him a wary glance and took a step back, yet for some unfathomable reason had the opposite effect on her. She wanted to invade his personal space and rub up against him to explore the terrain of his hard body. By the Gods, there didn't look to be an inch of softness about him.

At least there won't be if I have my way. A grin flirted with her lips at the very un-princess-like thought.

"Your Highness." He bent slightly at the waist. "I come with news."

The formality of his greeting was an unexpected splash of cold water.

Two years. Two years since she'd seen anyone from her kingdom. She had thought that once the guard had found her location, they would greet her like a long-lost sister. Apparently, that was not to be the case.

She shook off the disappointment and settled her hands on her hips. "What? No hello? I haven't seen you in years, and this is how you greet me?"

"Princess, if I can have a word with you in private. I have news of great importance I must impart to you."

"Of course it is, otherwise I'm certain you wouldn't be here."

Lucian batted at the confetti falling in his face and glanced pointedly at the encroaching dancers. "Please, let us retire to a more…quiet location."

As fast as a blink, the disapproval in his tone snapped her into the past where her father, or the court elders, looked upon her with icy contempt and an unveiled disbelief that she was actually one of their species. She shivered as a coldness she hadn't experienced since stepping into that spacecraft years before washed over her.

"Shall we?" Lucian gestured for her to precede him off the dance floor.

Amaryllis turned and took a timid step.

A million miles of distance, a different culture and a new identity. None of that mattered as in one breath she was once again that girl desperate to perform as was expected, all the while knowing she was going to fail miserably.

Wasn't time supposed to lessen the humiliation of the past? Didn't overcoming adversity strengthen one's spine and provide the fortitude to say "fuck you" in the face of public opinion? Where was that strength now, she wondered as her knees shook. Her high-heel wobbled and her ankle twisted as she stumbled back into a group of dancers.

"Amaryllis? Are you okay, honey?" asked one of the club's regulars. The woman leaned close to whisper, not so quietly, "Is this guy bothering you? I can get Angus to take care of him, no problem."

"I, um, I'm fine, thank you." Amaryllis straightened. "I've got this."

Yes, you've got this.

No longer was she the awkward princess. On this planet what made her different was admired, even loved. Men begged for the pleasure to share her bed and women longed to be her friend. She built a tiny empire by the sheer sweat of her own back. The Cavern was a haven where all who entered received what they needed and that included her.

What she needed now was to be cradled in the proverbial arms of those who loved her as she was. In the center of all this chaos she was in her element. She was strong because she brought all of these people together, they gave her courage and on the dance floor she would stay.

"Whatever you have to say can be said amongst friends."

Lucian closed his eyes as his hands fisted at his sides. "As the head of your guard, I request that you come with me now."

Wow, he barely moved his lips to grit that out. His refusal to loosen his formal constraint in even the slightest made her want to dig in her stilettos all the more. "No."

"If you—"

"No. This is my favorite song and I want to dance." She turned her back to him and gestured to the deejay to pump up the music.

Lucian stepped into her vision. "Your father is dead."

The blood froze in her veins before her two hearts kicked in her chest.

She had always wondered what she'd say or feel when she finally heard those words. Sorrow. Relief. Happiness? Now the time was nigh and all she felt was a vast expanse of nothing.

In a land where the people were tall, lean and dark, King Renauld had been bestowed with a short, round daughter with hair so blonde it looked silver and little control when it came to her emotions. Only his bond with her mother convinced him of her legitimacy.

And now he was dead.

If Lucian expected her to collapse in grief, he was bound for disappointment. She had mourned her former life and all it included during the long journey between worlds. There was no more left to grieve.

"Did he finally choke on his own arrogance?" Well, the grief was gone, but the bitterness lingered like rotten garlic.

He tilted his head and frowned. "That's uncalled for, Your Highness. He loved you dearly."

"Right." She chuckled without humor. "That is why I was sent to safety to the same place he found fit to be a prison for you and your brother."

"That was not his reason. He wanted you as far from danger as possible. I chose—" He pursed his lips and took a surreptitious glance around. "I chose here. I wanted to be close in case you had need of us."

If his earlier declaration had been a surprise, this bit of news had her downright gobsmacked. "In need of you? Yet I say again, I haven't seen you or your brother once since I received the missive you were banished to Earth, and it appears you've known my exact location this entire time. Why should I believe you?"

"Because it's the truth. Once I saw that you had established a life and were doing well, I thought it best to keep my distance."

Doing well? She guessed that compared to being beaten and disavowed, floundering around in a new culture entirely on one's own might be considered "doing well".

"Well, how kind of you to assume I wouldn't want to say hello to two men who once swore fealty to my family and protected us with their lives."

Confusion tightened his brow. "I meant no disrespect with my distance."

"For certain." She threw a thick blanket on her scattered emotions and strove for her most serene smile. "I thank you for your effort, General. It's been lovely to see you. Feel free to stop by again, perhaps under more pleasant circumstances."

He placed a hand on her arm and immediately pulled back, staring at his palm as if she burned him. He shook his head and said, "Your Highness, I have more news."

And didn't he sound excited. What more could there be? When she had gone into exile she had resigned herself on never returning home. With both of her parents dead, that infinitesimal spark of hope was effectively doused and was now nothing more than a soggy, smoldering pile of ash. And the fact she wanted to weep for that loss depressed her more than anything.

"If it's as jovial as the last, I don't think I want to hear it." No, all she wanted was to throw herself into the deepest well of human emotion and not think for a long, long time. "You've delivered your message. You may go."

"I insist to be heard."

"I don't want to hear it."

"Princess."

"Dance with me."

His eyes widened and he actually jumped a step backward. "What?"

Laughter welled in her chest at his reaction. One would think she asked him to drown kittens. "Dance with me. You have made me sad with this news. Make it up to me and dance."

"I don't dance."

To her surprise, the great General Lucianllanos actually looked terrified. Her inner devil jumped with glee at the opportunity to needle the stalwart soldier. Why should she be the only one to feel as if her skin was peeled back, leaving her exposed and raw? Besides, if he was insisting on treating her like a princess, then he could follow her orders.

She sashayed up to him and placed her hand on his chest, leaning into his rigid stance. "I've seen you during training exercises. You are very graceful. Pretend you're holding your sword." A quirk of naughtiness touched her grin. "And do what comes naturally."

The pink in his cheeks darkened. "I. Don't. Dance."

"Then I. Won't. Listen. It's obvious you wish to be gone from here post haste and as unobtrusively as possible. Do you realize you're a head taller than everyone here? And you are so stiff. You're like a giant tree in the midst of swaying reeds. How can you not be noticed?" She dug her fingers into the thick muscles of his shoulders and was immediately lost in the heat of his skin. Ah, what it would be like to feel that warmth without the barrier of fabric, perhaps even slick with sweat.

Focus. Focus.

"Relax. Drink in the energy around you. You give me one dance and I'll give you my complete attention."

His frown deepened as his hands landed on her hips and pushed her back enough to leave plenty of distance between their bodies. With a frustrated grunt, he began a step-touch, step-touch beat that reminded her of a youth at his first social dance.

"Bend your knees a little, Lucian. Follow the music. It's a dance, not a military march."

"I don't remember you being so disagreeable," he groused as he relaxed enough to soften his stance.

"I wasn't allowed to be. Demureness at all cost was the mantra I was expected to live by."

"Is decorum not something you adhere to here as well?"

"When it suits my purpose." She laughed. Had he always been such a... What did they call it here? A branch in the muck? Yes, that was Lucian. He needed a serious shot of excitement. "I find Earth-men like it when I behave contrary to what is expected. It keeps them on their toes."

His fingers flexed on her hips and a thin bolt of indignation burst through his controlled shell. "And what is it that these men expect from you?"

"Everything and anything."

"As a princess—"

"Do not even think of taking that tone with me, General. This isn't Skandavia. The old rules no longer apply."

"Be that as it may, but in some cases I will insist that they be. Princess, you are in danger."

"Unless it is from boredom, that is highly unlikely."

"Listen to me." He squeezed her tight, drawing her gaze to the intensity blazing in his dark-green eyes. "Hamerkind has the throne, but not the people. If you were to return, he would lose his control. He has sent an assassin to make sure you, my brother and myself do not return. I will not let him succeed."

Amaryllis melted at the command in his tone. The show of strength pushed all of the submissive buttons she tried to deny possessing. She licked her dry lips and shoved aside the desire to kneel at his feet and await his instruction. "That's ridiculous. As if I have any intention of returning. How can this man even think the people will accept my leadership after the way they treated me like an abomination?" She snapped her teeth together and squashed the anger that flared at the reminder of her past. "I will tell this assassin that his services are unnecessary and he will go."

Lucian's bark of laughter was so loud, it startled them both. "Now who is being ridiculous? Bale is a cold-blooded killer. He will not let you live long enough to draw a breath, let alone form an argument."

"I do not know this Bale."

"I do. And he's dangerous. You need to come with me. I will protect you."

"And why should I trust you? You've completely ignored me."

"That is not true. I told you I've kept track of you. I've even dined in your restaurant a time or two."

"A time or two?" Now that was surprising. Why monitor her whereabouts without letting her know? "Then why haven't you spoken to me?"

"Because I couldn't—" He paused, his throat working hard as he swallowed. "I…didn't want to intrude on your new life. You've done quite well for yourself, Your Highness."

"Despite all the odds?"

"Yes."

"Yet you don't approve of all my endeavors."

He glanced around the club again and at the mass of undulating bodies crowding ever so closer. His lips pressed into a firm line and he drew her into the curve of his body as if to shield her from their touch. "Not all of them. You let others take too many liberties where you are concerned."

"Liberties?" She laughed and rubbed her cheek against his slightly stubbled jaw. The scrape sent tiny chills across her skin. "You make it sound so pedestrian. I like liberties. Come on, General. Haven't you ever done anything just for the pleasure, for the pure excitement of feeling your blood race?"

He opened his mouth to argue but paused when she raised a brow. "Maybe. In my youth. But never as a mature member of society."

"Poor Lucian. What is the human saying? All work and no play makes a man limp and feeble?"

His nostrils flared. "I am neither."

"One dance, Lucian." She barely contained her smile. "You promised me one dance. Don't do anything but feel the energy around us."

Amaryllis drew his enticing scent of pine and musk into her lungs then released a sigh of possibility. Lucian was so uptight, so formal. What a magnificent sight he would make if he unleashed the primal male she sensed lurking beneath the layer of responsibility.

The deep throb of bass pounded behind her chest as she let the music take her over. Lucian easily supported her weight, swaying and rolling with her movements and the driving primal beat. His steps were smooth, graceful and in perfect tempo. Liar, he did know how to dance.

He was so warm, his body generated enough heat to make a fine layer of sweat gather in her cleavage. A drop of perspiration slipped under the silk of her dress and tickled her skin as it slid down her belly. With each bob and weave their bodies fused together, surging in a gentle cadence. She stifled a moan when his thigh slipped between her legs and pressed against the ache growing in her core.

Oh if only they were naked. She snorted with repressed

laughter, if only they weren't who they presently were.

Closing her eyes, she pictured another version of Amaryllis and Lucian. One where he was cuffed to the wall, unable to prevent her from touching him anywhere and everywhere she desired. Or perhaps she would allow him to take the lead, letting him wield his authority to drive her to absolute mindlessness.

The thought of allowing another to overpower her frightened her as much as it had her near orgasm. She ground her pussy against the firm muscles of his thigh, her breath grew faster as her stomach clenched tighter and tighter. His fingers dug into her flesh before he slid his hands lower, cupping her buttocks as he curled around her.

On the edge of the dance floor, a couple caught her attention. The woman was fair and light while her male companion was as dark as cocoa. He had her back pressed to his front, his broad hand a stark contrast to the creamy skin of the breast he pulled from the bodice of her dress and massaged with long fingers. Her skirt was hiked to her waist and with each thrust of his hips, her mouth fell open on a cry. By the strain thinning his lips, Amaryllis knew the woman was getting a delicious fucking.

Would Lucian ever take a woman so publicly? Say "fuck decorum" and sate his hungers because he could not wait one more second to have her howling beneath him?

With that thought her temperature rose as the heat and lusts of the pressing crowd fed her arousal. The lips of her sex grew slick and her nipples tightened where they were pressed flush against his hard chest. Along her thigh his erection lengthened, making her mouth water at the thought of how he'd feel sliding into her mouth. Gods did she want to taste him. Savor his flavor and suckle his cock until he lost that tightly leashed control.

The brush of his lips against her neck made her shiver and her head tip back, ready to accept the kiss she could already feel bruising her lips.

"Lucian," she sighed and gazed up into his drowsy green eyes.

Awareness dilated his pupils as he drew a sharp breath.

"No." He wrenched her away from him so hard, she stumbled in her heels. His eyes blazed and his features turned to granite. "No. You cannot think of me that way."

Shame exploded in her chest, stealing the rest of her breath as flames of embarrassment scorched her cheeks. That's right. He was the well-respected head of the royal guard and she was the improper princess who couldn't control her emotions. She wasn't allowed to feel anything.

With as much self-respect as she could muster, she threw back her shoulders and lifted her chin. "You message has been delivered, General. You are dismissed."

Pity filled his eyes as he lifted a hand in supplication. "Amaryllis."

The sound of her given name on his lips battered her defenses. "Go, Lucianllanos. I command you."

His lips tightened and an argument gathered in his eyes, but he bent at the hips and turned, disappearing into the crowd.

The general may have left without protest, but he would not be gone for long. He truly believed there was a threat to her safety, and he was *Llanos*. His honor dictated he protect her. No matter how she might wish otherwise.

She looked neither to the left nor right as she made her way to the staircase sweeping up to her private room. No need to see the condoling expressions on whoever witnessed her humiliation.

Her knees were still weak from Lucian's embrace, which only angered her all the more. Despite his protest, he had not been immune to her closeness. The impression of the solid erection he pressed along her thigh made it clear he was very interested in blurring the line between servant and master. What bothered her now was the question of whether he was the stronger one to put an immediate end to an affair probably destined to end in a flaming blaze of disaster, or was he a coward for not being willing to take a chance on the potential of something special.

Didn't matter now, she rationalized. Lucian was never going to allow her to get that close to him again, and she refused to waste energy on bending the unbendable.

With each step toward her convictions, her feet dragged as if weighted in concrete and not her strappy Louboutins. She had forgotten how exhausting it was to continually lock down her emotions. What she loved most about this new world was the freedom to feel what she wanted when she wanted. Lucian's rejection was a clear reminder of everything she hated about her former life, and his reaction stung like a cut from a knife dipped in acid.

The bouncer at the foot of the stairs moved the velvet rope for her as she approached.

"Do not let anyone unfamiliar up these stairs," she murmured to her man. "Use whatever means necessary. That goes for every area of the club. Spread the word, please."

"Yes ma'am."

Just because she was angry at Lucian didn't mean she was stupid. The threat was real and she'd take the appropriate precautions.

As she entered the skyloft, the pounding music of the dance floor faded and was replaced with the rhythmic sound of flesh meeting flesh, punctuated by a guttural moan.

Amaryllis wove through the various couplings to her throne of buttery white leather and velvet pillows. The loveseat was so deep, she could easily lie flat on her back if she so wished.

In front of her a woman was laid facedown over an ottoman. Dressed only in the studded cuffs that bound her wrists and ankles, she made a stunning picture framed by the blond drilling his cock into her mouth and the brunet who took her pussy with hard, quick thrusts that matched his partner's.

Normally this type of tableau would be exactly what she

craved. Now the euphoria permeating the air depressed her. How she admired the woman's ability to let go and not care what people thought about her, not care that her flanks rippled and breasts bounced. She was in the moment, and Amaryllis envied her like no other.

The couch bounced as another body flopped down next to her.

"What's wrong?" her new companion asked.

Ah Jorges. She should have known her best friend would seek her out at her weakest moment.

"Nothing." She jumped up, only to pause as her head swam. Absorbing all the intense emotions swirling around the loft was like a smoker taking a hit and not exhaling. Without the blessed relief of release, she was ready to snap, and she didn't need an audience to witness another humiliation. Since a princess never hurried, she sashayed toward the balcony.

As she expected, Jorges followed on her heels. "Bullshit and I think it has something to do with that massive hunk of beefcake I saw you dancing with earlier. Who is he?"

"Just someone I know. No one special."

"Puh-leaze. We treat you like a princess because you're the best and we love you, but he treated you like royalty. I think I actually saw him bow. And that dance. You two were ablaze and it spread like wildfire. I'm surprised more people aren't fucking on the dance floor."

The fact that Jorges noticed the heat Lucian denied did not make her feel better.

She crossed to the floor-to-ceiling windows that allowed her to see out, but kept others from seeing in, and looked to the floor below as if through Lucian's eyes.

A clash of humanity. Dark. Sin spilling from the shadows. A cave of debauchery and vice where responsibility was dumped at the door and rules touched with a match to burn to ashes. It was a wonder he bothered to step across the threshold at all.

She looked to her friend and wondered. Jorges was a handsome man, vibrant and healthy with wheat-colored hair tipped with gold and laughing blue eyes. He had a lean, swimmer's physique and tawny skin. An intricate scrollwork tattoo, which she knew ran down the length of his torso to curl around the base of his cock, peeked above the collar of his white t-shirt. It was a design she'd traced with her tongue many times.

Was that wrong? Was it a bad thing to take pleasure from another with no expectation of forging a lasting commitment? To engage in an activity for the pure pleasure of feeling and nothing more? Did that make her an awful person? An hour before the answer would have been fuck no, but now…

"What have we become, Jorges?" she whispered. "Is all that we are only about sex?"

"You're scaring me, Amaryllis. What are you talking about? You love sex. Shit, you've built this entire place in glory of it." He looked at her in horror. "Why are you crying?"

"I'm not." She swiped the tears from her eyes. He had spoken the truth, mostly. "Was this wrong? Am I a bad person because I encourage people to explore their sexuality and am not using my money to solve a greater social issue?"

"Come here, honey." He pulled her into a hug. "I don't know what's gotten into you, but you're talking crazy. And believe me, there is no bigger social issue than people dealing with their sexuality. When you asked me to design this club, the one thing you insisted on was that anyone who walked through that door was welcome and should immediately feel at home. Has it become the number-one sex destination in the northwest? Yes, but that's because you've done what you set out to do. Make people feel comfortable in their own skin. Explore the side of their personality they're too afraid to explore in their normal environment. That is a gift, Amaryllis. You used to be proud of that."

She tightened her arms around his waist. "You're right. I was. I am. I guess I was looking too hard at my life through my eyes and not my heart. Thank you for being a good friend."

"I love you." He kissed the top of her head. "You're my hero. It makes me sad to see you question your successes. Why do I get the feeling this bout of self-doubt has something to do with your mystery man? Tell me, who was that guy?"

Jorges deserved the truth. Or at least what little she could offer. Under his sinful exterior beat a compassionate heart, which was one of the many things she loved about him. If he were to be injured by someone trying to get to her, she'd be devastated.

"That man is from my homeland and once worked for my

father. He brought me news that my father has been killed and his enemies may be after me."

"Holy shit. Are you serious?"

Chills ran up her arms as she considered the possibilities. "It is conceivable."

He grasped her hand and placed a kiss into her palm. "I thought you left Sweden to get away from the dangers of your father's job. Hey, was that guy in the mob too?"

She hid a smile at his mention of her cover story. "No, he guarded my father after he went into witness protection. Please, don't worry. I'm sure there isn't any real danger, but all the same, I want you to be on the lookout for anyone suspicious."

Jorges slid his arm around her waist and pressed a kiss to her shoulder. "Maybe you should leave town, lie low for a while."

"I'm not going to live my life in hiding, Jorges."

"But you'll be safe. And…by the frown on your face I have a feeling you just had this same argument."

"Intuitive you are."

"Promise that you'll leave town at the first sign of trouble."

"I promise."

"Good. I'll hold you to it." He stroked his hand down her back, digging his thumbs into the tense muscles. "No wonder you've been out of sorts. What you need is a night of pampering and orgasms. Let's go to your place."

An hour earlier she would have said yes and dragged him

back to her apartment by his cock. Now the idea left her ice cold. "That sounds lovely, but perhaps another night."

"There must be something I can do to make you happy."

Jorges was so sincere in his desire to please, she refused to let her sour mood trample his need. "Do you really want to make me happy?"

"Always."

She pointed at a spot on the other side of the glass. "Do you see that woman sitting alone at the bar?"

"Yes."

"I want you to dance with her."

His brow creased with confusion. "Why?"

"Because she needs to."

"And you know this how?"

Amaryllis smiled. She had noticed the woman earlier in the evening. Two empty martini glasses sat in front of her as she nursed a third. Every once in a while she would tug at the new blouse that exposed a fair amount of cleavage and glance longingly at the couples on the dance floor. There was an air of fragility about her that screamed she had been hurt before. It was her courage of coming to a place that obviously evoked a fear of the unknown that drew Amaryllis' attention and admiration.

"Let's say it's one woman sympathizing with another. Dance with her."

Jorges leaned forward for another look. "She's pretty enough, I guess. A little plain."

"Don't look with only your eyes." She twisted his nipple through his shirt in reprimand. "She wants to shine but is afraid. See how her hand trembles? Can you not feel her desire to join? I want you to dance with her. That would make me happy."

An amused smile curled his lips. "How does that please you?"

"Because every woman deserves to feel as if she is the most beautiful thing in existence, to feel wanted. Something tells me she has not had that experience. I want you to make her not regret coming to my club. You make her happy, then I will be happy."

He glanced back at the woman with a new respect lighting his features. "I will give her a night she will never forget."

She kissed his cheek. "Thank you, my friend."

Amaryllis waited by the window until she saw Jorges approach Ms. Lonely Heart. At first the woman looked ready to bolt when he attempted to strike up a conversation, but he turned up the charm and soon she released a smile so brilliant, she outshone the brightest star.

Satisfied that she helped at least one person fulfill their deepest desires, Amaryllis made her way to her apartment situated above the club. Her feet hurt and her dress began to stick to her skin in the most unpleasant way. What she needed was a hot bath and a long time with her favorite toy. Please may she have enough batteries on hand.

Chapter Three

THE BAY DOOR opened, revealing a light so brilliant it brought Bale to his knees. He pulled the hood of his cloak down over his watering eyes and stepped into the knee-high grass. To his left was hill after hill of waving gold reeds. To his right ran a stream bordered by trees with deep-green-and-yellow leaves that dazzled against the blue sky. By the Gods, he had thought such color only existed in his dreams.

He held out his hand in the sunlight and marveled at the concentration of heat that warmed his skin. Under his heavy cloak his body began to perspire. How odd. Who would have thought one could break a sweat without exerting any energy.

The brief bout of amusement brought a frown to his lips. He was not sent to explore this new world nor was this a vacation. The only joy to be found was in succeeding on his mission.

Turning his back on the magnificent view, he took stock of the munitions and equipment that survived the fall to Earth. The pod itself sustained the most damage, but had the potential to make the return trip if he located the necessary supplies.

Return to Skandavia? Now there was a novel thought.

A low, rumbling growl interrupted his inspection. Bale

stepped around his craft to see a vehicle approach. The front cabin looked large enough for two, yet only held one, and the flatbed was empty. He kept a hand over the grip of his blaster and planted his feet in a battle-ready stance as the truck came to a stop.

The driver opened the door and stepped out. "Just what do you think you're doing there, boy? You destroyed my wheat."

Bale looked at the trail of scorched grain that led to his space craft. "My apologies."

The grizzled farmer spat a stream of brown juice at his feet. "Apologies don't mean shit." He raised a long-barreled rifle and aimed it at his chest. "Now get your machine and get the hell off my farm."

Bale drew his blaster and fired, hitting the man in the hand and knocking the rifle to the ground. He pulled the trigger again and nothing. The heat from the sun must have vaporized the gases that formed the bullets. He threw the useless piece of metal aside and ran for his target. Before he could blink, he was at the man's side, twisting his thin arm and breaking the frail bone.

Shock held Bale immobile. *Ack jus.* What was this sorcery? How was it possible to move with such quickness? He had barely touched the human, yet caused much injury.

Mental reasoning suggested that humans, as a whole, were weak, however Bale sensed that something was definitely different about his body. Colors were sharper, his hearing more acute and his empathetic abilities were bombarded with the man's fear that was as acrid as the scent of the urine he wet himself with. Yes, these heightened abilities would have to be more closely examined. But not now.

"Where am I?" he asked.

"On my farm," the man wheezed.

"What colony?"

"Colony?" Under Bale's hand, the old heart beat a frantic rhythm.

"The name."

"Waitsburg."

"How far are we from the city?"

"'Bout five hours' drive."

Bale shifted his hold to around the man's throat. "Do you have a shelter?"

The man blinked rapidly and tried to nod.

"You will take me there and give me what I need to continue my journey. If you breathe one word of my existence to any living thing, I will slaughter every person within this colony. Do you understand?"

"Yes. Yes."

Satisfied that his word would be obeyed, Bale stood and returned to his craft. He glanced at his hands then at the heavy module. Was it possible?

He dug his boots into the earth and bent his knees. Grasping the egg-shaped craft at the base, he lifted the pod off the ground. It was heavy, no doubt, but not unmanageable. He carried it to the flatbed of the truck and set it down. The tires sank into the dirt under the extreme weight.

Yes, this unexpected development was most certainly something that deserved his utmost consideration.

✦   ✦   ✦

"IF YOU WISH to keep that finger, I suggest you stop pressing that damn button," Amaryllis shouted as she stumbled down the hall.

Good mother take her, she hadn't slept one wink and a headache throbbed behind her eyes. She wished she could blame her hungover state on a night of drunken revelry, but since she hadn't touched a drop of liquor the night before and had even gone to bed relatively early, the fault lay squarely on one thing. Specifically, one man. All night long her body ached and no matter how many orgasms she gave herself, satisfaction never came. Visions of a certain green-eyed warrior who smoldered with lust one moment then froze over with disdain the next tormented her, waking and sleeping.

She tightened the belt of her robe and threw open the door and found the cause of her sleepless night standing on her doorstep. He stood in the obligatory hardass stance with his arms folded across his chest. His frown was so deep you could fill it with water and irrigate ten ranches for years.

"Bang-bang, you're dead," Lucian said. "How could you open the door without checking to see who it is? You are making it too easy to kill you."

"I will gladly accept death, if it means being away from

you," she spat.

He jerked back as if she slapped him. His lips tightened and a veil fell across his features as he nodded. "I'm going to ignore that remark because you look as if you are not feeling well and we did not part on the best of terms last night."

How dare he mention her bedraggled state! But he was right, loath that she was to admit. Snippy behavior might make her feel better for the moment, but she was a princess. If no longer in name, than at least in disposition. With the great wunderkind looking down his nose at her, she was going to have to be extra diligent controlling her emotions.

"To what do I owe this pleasure?" she asked with a lift of her chin.

"I've brought a visitor, if you're up for an audience."

"Who?" She stood on tiptoe to see around his massive biceps and screeched with joy when she saw the man standing in front of the elevator. "Dhavin!"

All thoughts of decorum disappeared like a cube of sugar in the rain as she ran full bore and leapt into the arms of her former personal guard. Dhavin laughed and swung her around twice before setting her on her feet.

"Oh how I've missed you." She planted a kiss on his lips that was in no way brotherly. His hips pressed into her belly before he pulled back with a gasp.

A burning flush of angry heat raced up her back. Oh was the big, bad general upset? Hmm, the idea of spending the day irritating the great Lucianllanos was greatly appealing.

"Thank you for the welcome." Dhavin leaned close and gritted out, "Are you trying to have me killed?"

"Don't all women have a soft spot for their first lover?" Another hot flash lashed at her. How delicious. She threw Dhavin a saucy wink and pulled him over the threshold. "When did you arrive? Where are you staying? Oh there are so many wonderful things to show you about this world."

"This is not a social visit, Your Highness." Lucian shot a daggered glare at Dhavin as he locked the door behind them. "We are here on matters of importance."

She heaved a deep sigh. "Fine. Please, join me in the sitting room."

Their thick-soled boots thumped on the hardwood floor behind her. Their steps were measured in perfect synchronization, heavy and purposeful, a testament to their years of training side by side.

Amaryllis delicately sat upon a velvet-upholstered French antique throne chair and crossed her legs. The action split the cloth of her robe to her hip, leaving no doubt she wore nothing under the lavender silk.

Not a word was spoken as both men took a moment to caress her with their gazes. Dhavin with appreciation, and Lucian, ah… Heat and wanton hunger sizzled over her skin, tightening her nipples to hard points that scraped against the soft fabric. Just as quickly as the sensation flared, it disappeared.

"Your Highness," Lucian began with a rough crackle. He

stopped to clear his throat and tried again. "Your Highness, I can afford you a few minutes, if you wish to go dress."

"Oh no. You said this was important." She swept her hand out and turned it palm up. "*Gram* Dhavinllanos, you may begin."

He stared at her with wide eyes and shook his head as if to ask if she were insane to push the general's buttons. He dropped to one knee with a grin tugging at the corners of his mouth, then he stood and bowed at the waist. "Princess Amaryllis. I offer my condolences on the loss of your father."

She nodded at his gesture. "Thank you."

"I apologize that I bring more distressing news. You are in grave danger. Hamerkind will not rest until his crown is secure. The assassin who has been sent for you is ruthless. Bale is a soulless killer with no reason to live. He will go after you with everything he has."

"Yes, so Lucian informed me last eve." A snick of memory tickled her subconscious. "Bale. Why does that name sound familiar to me now?"

"He was part of your father's retinue," Lucian answered.

Her brow rose with surprise. "And now he's committed to kill the very thing he once fought for the honor of defending?"

"Yes."

"Why?"

A dark flush graced his cheek. "He lost what he once held dear. But the why is not the point. You will come with us to safety until the threat is eliminated."

The quick change of subject did not go unnoticed. So, the great general was hiding a secret. Very intriguing. The mere fact she found it intriguing annoyed the blazes out of her. She didn't want to find anything fascinating about the man.

She turned back to Dhavin. "What is your proposal concerning this assassin?"

"Well." He snuck a quick glance at Lucian before answering, "We will take you to Cedar. It's a little colony not far from here, but fairly remote. You will be under the care of Kristos and his mated wife."

"Kristos has bonded?" The news had her sitting upright with not only surprise but a touch of envy. "He bonded with a human?"

"Yes. Brett is the sheriff. She will be able to help in your—"

"Imprisonment," she finished for him. "Call a spade a spade. You want to lock me away. But why do you want to risk people you care for by bringing danger to them?"

"We will be protecting you from an advantageous location," Lucian interjected. "You will stay safe and protected until Bale is dealt with. Then you may return."

"For how long will I remain in custody?"

"For as long as it takes."

"I see," she drew out slowly. "No."

His cheeks flushed red as he shouted, "You cannot say no."

"I can do whatever I want." She rose to her feet. "All you have is information that this Bale is after me, but do you have proof that he survived the journey?"

"Not yet."

"Have you seen him?"

The muscles in his jaw twitched. "We saw what looked like a craft falling to Earth the same night Dhavin landed."

"But you haven't seen him in person?" She held up her hand when she saw him gather steam. "I have too many responsibilities, too many people counting on me to just disappear for an undetermined amount of time. When you have gathered more substantial information and have a plan that involves more than me sitting on my ass in the forest, then we can speak of this again. Now, if you'll excuse me, I'm going to bathe. I won't be but a few minutes, and I do wish to visit with you, Dhavin. There is melon in the refrigerator and a lovely prosciutto. Please, make yourselves comfortable." She paused to glance at both men over her shoulder. "If I need assistance, I know who not to call for."

LUCIAN STOOD TRANSFIXED by the swish of the princess's hips under the shimmering robe. After she disappeared from sight, he snapped back into the present. Dhavin, however, continued to look after her with an appreciative gleam in his eyes. The knowing smirk on the other man's lips set Lucian off. He raced across the room and slammed his cousin into the wall.

"You had sexual relations with the princess?" he growled.

"Get. Off me. Cousin," Dhavin gasped, struggling with the arm digging across his windpipe.

"You had sex with the princess?" he roared. "How stupid

could you be?"

"Get off." Dhavin jammed two fingers under his ribs, followed with a punch to the kidneys. Once free he rubbed at this throat. "Amaryllis can be very persuasive when she wants something. At the time, she wanted me."

Lucian reached out and grabbed nothing but a fistful of air as Dhavin ducked to safety. "Were you insane? If you had been discovered, you would have been executed."

"She needed me!" He checked over his shoulder, then took a step closer to whisper in a harsh tone, "As her guard it is my job to provide for her, and she needed me. You were so wrapped up with the king, you've no idea what life was like for her. She wasn't afforded the respect due her position, and it was completely undeserved."

"But the rules—"

"Are sometimes worthless. Do not condemn her or me without knowing all the facts, cousin. What Amaryllis and I had was special, but also much in the past. She is my friend. Let me speak with her. I'll convince her to come with us."

It galled Lucian to admit, although it was only to himself, that his cousin may be right. It was obvious he rubbed her the wrong way. The hurt she felt at his rejection the night before still stung where it had pierced his heart.

The wide-eyed, introspective girl he remembered had been replaced with a sex bomb with devious tendencies. She was unlike any woman he'd ever met, in either world. The difference went beyond the long fall of white-blonde hair and the fathomless lavender eyes that appeared to hold the answers to his darkest fantasies. She was fearless and intelligent. A frightening combination in his opinion.

And how could he not think about those curves? They had beguiled more than one man on Skandavia, including him, if he was truthful. At the time he had valued his position more than his libido and refused to dwell on such thoughts. But now he was entranced by her breasts and hips that were so lush, his palms itched to be filled with all that flesh and immerse himself in her softness. Sinking his cock into her had been the last thing he thought about before a restless night's sleep and the first thing to wake him up with a raging erection that still hadn't ceased. If she only knew how badly he wanted to give in to the temptation of her full lips, she'd probably...well, she'd probably do every wicked thing he asked, which was not going to keep her safe.

At all cost, he must maintain his control.

"Make her see reason."

Dhavin nodded. "I'll do my best. She can be quite a handful."

Lucian stopped him before he left the room. Though it wasn't his business, he had to know. "Was she worth the risk?"

He looked in the direction of the princess's room. A slow smile curled his lips when he turned back to Lucian. "For certain."

Sincerity rang from his words like a tap on the finest crystal. Envy the likes Lucian never imagined coiled around his chest, squeezing the air from his lungs. In his mind's eye visions of his cousin and the princess rolling around naked on any available flat surface burned his brain.

A shaft of lust speared from his gut down to his cock. The reaction was ridiculous and entirely inappropriate. He had to get his mind off the beautiful princess and on to eliminating the danger stalking them.

A modulate ring emitted from his pocket. Lucian retrieved his phone and immediately pressed the green receiver button when he saw Kristos' name. "What happened?

✦　　✦　　✦

"WHAT DID HE do?"

Amaryllis glanced over her shoulder to see Dhavin leaning against the open doorway of her room with his arms crossed.

She batted her lashes and innocently pouted. "Whatever are you talking about?"

He rolled his eyes and stepped deeper into the room. "My cousin is the most in-control man ever created and he is now acting like a cork under extreme pressure. And you, little witch, are the fingers trying to pry him loose. What did he do?"

She gave an elegant shrug of her shoulder. "He was just being his usual bossy, arrogant, *boarhound*-ass that I remember. He thinks he can give orders and I will obey as if we were at home. I suppose he will have to learn the hard way that circumstances are much different here than on Skandavia."

"I'm getting the impression that you are going to enjoy every tortuous moment of his lessons."

Her grin brightened for a moment before she tempered the relish that flared when she thought about sparring with the general. "I'm going to do my best to ignore him."

"Of course," he replied in a tone that spoke of exactly how much he believed that.

He gestured to her grand four-poster bed with red-and-orange drapery and the mahogany Chippendale settee with fat fluffy pillows nestled in the corners. "Your home is amazing. It's so inviting and warm. You really love it here, don't you?"

"Oh Dhavin, I do," she sighed. "There is so much color, so much life, especially here in America. Don't get me wrong, there are ugly parts, much as there is ugliness in every colony, but here, almost anything is possible. It's my home now."

His smile matched the brilliance shining in his eyes. "When you disappeared, I knew it was not for ill. I hoped that wherever you were sent, you would find happiness. And look at you now. I hear you're quite the entrepreneur. A restaurant and a nightclub. Very ambitious."

"They have the most amazing food here, and I wanted to be a part of that, so I opened a restaurant. What have you eaten since you've arrived? Have you tried vegetables? There are so many different varieties. And dessert. There is an entire course devoted entirely to sweets."

"And what about relationships? Do you have a lover to share these experiences with?"

"I have several." She tossed him a wink as she went into the closet to find some accessories. "The men at my club have you to thank for their pleasure."

"You were an excellent student." The curl of his smile reminded her of the heat they used to generate. "I am sorely tempted to have you give me a personal tour of that club of yours. But I know of at least one person who would gladly cut my cock off if I mention it."

"He can't cut it off if it's in my mouth," she teased, knowing he'd never take her up on the offer if she asked. When the illicitness of their relationship had worn off, they realized they made better friends than lovers.

His eyes widened at her bold statement. "You are so bad."

"And you love me that way."

He tapped her on the tip of her nose. "I do."

The truth in those two words rang clear and strong. Dhavin knew her better than anyone and never hesitated to tell her how he loved all that she was. He was the one person in the universe she felt free to be one hundred percent herself with, and the unexpected freedom that came with that knowledge brought tears to her eyes.

She leapt into his arms. "I'm so glad you're here."

Like always, Dhavin caught her.

In the stormy waters of court and propriety he was the anchor that put all her troubles into perspective. He held her when she cried, laughed when she dared to say something funny and forced her to see the beauty in her body where she had only seen flaws and differences from those she was held against to be an example to. He taught her passion and gave her an outlet to express her needs. He was a true friend, and it wasn't until he walked through her door that she realized how much she missed having his companionship.

"What are you doing?"

The disapproval in the question matched the severity of Lucian's frown. Dhavin stiffened, but she clung on tighter, allowing the warm ripple of pleasure she felt in the simple embrace fill the air.

"It's called a hug, General. Perhaps you haven't experienced one before. It's what you do when you wish to express affection."

"Play nice," Dhavin husked then swatted her on the rear. He turned toward his cousin and stiffened at her side. "What is wrong?"

"Kristos called. Brett received word that a debris trail was located in eastern Washington. There was no craft, but a quarter-mile swath of wheat field was destroyed. The landowner was questioned. He was wearing a sling and sported bruises, and was exorbitantly adamant that he witnessed nothing unusual."

"Bale," Dhavin growled.

For the first time in years, Amaryllis tasted the bitter bile of true fear. It was not the first time her life had been threatened, but she had foolishly believed that the practice of constantly fearing for her life was long over. And why? Because of the potential threat she was to a man who lived millions of miles away. The injustice of it all had the well of rage seething inside her.

"Princess, I said you must come with us," Lucian barked, oblivious that she was in her own head.

"I know," she shouted. She was independent, not stupid. "I have never doubted the seriousness of the situation, General. I understand the danger and will go with you. You have three moons to eliminate the assassin before I return to my home."

"Three?" His nostrils flared as he crossed his arms over his huge chest. "Unacceptable."

"I also did not exaggerate my responsibilities. I have people who depend on me for their livelihoods and I cannot simply disappear for an undetermined length of time. As it is, it will be a challenge to arrange for my absence on such short notice. Three moons is all I can afford. Is this Bale such a formidable opponent that three *Llanos* cannot defeat him?"

"Dhavin. I need a moment with the princess. Alone. Please."

As her personal guard, Dhavin obeyed her will above all and waited for her approval before he made a move for the door. "I'll be close if you have need of me."

"Thank you, Dhavin." Amaryllis straightened her spine. Never would she show a weakness to this man. "I ask you again, General. Are you and your men not up to the task?"

"We are. But we have to be cautious. I need to know that you are protected at all times."

"So you plan to have me tied and submit to your wishes the entire time?"

His breath caught and a spike of arousal arced across the room to ignite a blaze in her womb as her powers soaked in the hungers he fought to control and hide from her.

Ah, so her general *did* want her tied and subservient to his desires. What would it take to get him to loosen his restraint and give in to those needs?

"Is that it, Lucian? Do you want me under your...thumb to protect me, or for another purpose?"

A slash of red stole across his cheeks. "My job is to see to your safety."

"And I will be oh so safe if I'm within arm's reach, won't I?"

Amazing, she thought, as the heat of his gaze fueled the flames that raced up her body to lick at the undersides of her breasts. She stalked closer and almost smiled as he staggered and backed into the wall behind him. "Is that the only reason you want me close, Lucian?"

His hands fell on her shoulders to stop her momentum. "Don't think you can manipulate me as easily as you do Dhavin."

She flinched. "You bastard. I've never manipulated anyone."

His fingers tightened as she moved to draw away. "Stop. I'm sorry. I'm sorry." He closed his eyes and let loose with a long sigh. "Why can't we hold a reasonable conversation?

Every time I try to talk to you, I end up hurting your feelings and that is never my intention."

"Maybe it's because you insist on treating me as someone that I'm not." She leaned into his chest and released her own sigh as the big man shuddered against her. The headiness of the danger of being so close to such tightly leashed control made her dizzy. "Why can't you see that?"

A mirthless chuckle rumbled in his chest. His hands slid down her back in a slow sweep then curled around her shoulders again. "What I see is a powder keg of trouble. You—you are unchartered territory, Your Highness."

"And I frighten you." She smiled at the discovery as his hips pressed into her belly. Oh yes, his body knew what he wanted, yet he was going to do everything in his power to fight his attraction.

"I'm an adult woman, Lucian. I know exactly what, and who, I want. What about you?"

He trembled again. His throat worked as he struggled for the words. "What I want doesn't matter."

"It does to me," she whispered.

His sigh ghosted across her lips as he bent his head closer. He pressed his forehead to hers and breathed in her scent on a deep inhale before gently pushing her away. "I am your guard. My sword will always be yours when you have need."

A wide grin stretched her lips as a delightful red flush raced up his neck to the tips of his ears as he realized how she interpreted his statement.

"I mean, to protect you. That is all I can give."

For now.

The unspoken words hung on the air between them.

As she looked upon Lucian with new eyes, the humiliation she suffered the night before dissipated.

Maybe it was his strength, maybe it was his honor, maybe it was the potential pleasure to be found in those massive hands, whatever it was, Lucian intrigued her like no other. She wanted to peel away his armor and experience the man hiding within. The general needed a challenge, and the one thing she excelled at was giving people exactly what they needed.

"If we are done now, General. I need to make arrangements for my time off, and I still haven't had my bath yet, so if you'll excuse me."

With a twist of her fingers, the lavender silk pooled at her feet. She sashayed to the bathroom with an extra swish of her hips.

Those flares of heat washing over her back were becoming incredibly addictive.

LUCIAN STARED AT the princess's delectable backside with his mouth agape until she closed the bathroom door between them with a knowing smile on her pouty lips. He pressed the heel of his hand into the erection threatening to bust through the zipper of his jeans and stifled a moan.

Damn the woman! Did she not know she was asking him to tackle her to the tile floor and feed the throbbing length of his cock into her pussy, whether she was ready for him or not?

Yes, the little witch did.

The princess was playing with an explosive that would burn them both. This all-consuming need to savor her ripeness was a thousand times more unbearable than it had been on Skandavia. At least then he had the overseeing eye of her father and his other duties to temper the fascination, but Amaryllis in her gloriously bare flesh was too much to withstand up close and personal. And he was not unaware of the fact that she was going to make the time they spent together very personal.

No! He would not think of his charge in such a manner. They may not be in Skandavia anymore, but she was still royalty and he, her servant. Keeping her safe was his top priority.

The sound of water flowing from pipes drew his attention to the flimsy door and he thought of a very naked princess on the other side.

He raced from the room with his hands clenched at his sides and went in search of a moment of privacy.

Dhavin was in the living room, his attention riveted to the large-screen television. The remote was in his hand and he was laughing as the channels flipped in rapid succession. A pair of breasts flashed across the screen and Dhavin switched back to the channel that showed two women frolicking in a swimming pool.

He sank on the ottoman and scooted closer to the action.

"I love this planet."

Lucian backtracked and found sanctuary in the kitchen. Why he thought the space would be full of stainless steel and cold tile was another example of how little he knew about Amaryllis. The warm wood and creamy granite was as inviting as the woman was outrageous.

He unbuttoned the cuff of his shirt around his left wrist and pulled the fabric back to his elbow. He turned the knob of the stove until the flame ignited, rising tall and white hot. With a deep breath of fortitude, he held his forearm over the fire. The stench of burning hair made his eyes water, but he held firm, biting back a howl of pain. His honor demanded he be at his best. Anything else was unacceptable.

Chapter Four

"**L**OOK AT THAT!" Amaryllis pointed out her window. Against the bright-blue sky gliders in brilliant reds and yellow spiraled gently from the cliffs down to a wide-open field. "Have you ever seen anything so amazing? Lucian, you must take me."

He glanced over his shoulder at her with a raised brow before he turned his attention back to the road. "No."

Big surprise there. "Dhavin, you'll take me, surely."

"I'm not too certain." He gazed up with trepidation from his seat in the front of the car. "I don't think I can trust a bit of colored fabric to prevent me from plunging to the earth."

"Where is your courage? I thought you two were *Llanos*? I bet you wouldn't even go bungee jumping with me."

"Do I want to know what that is?"

"A giant elastic band is tied to your waist or ankles, and then you jump off a high bridge. Just when you think you will crash upon the rocks, the elastic snaps you back and you go up and down until your momentum stops."

Dhavin's pallor took on a greenish tinge. "That sounds dreadful."

"Oh it's great fun." She leaned forward and poked her head

between the two sets of broad shoulders. "The adrenaline rush is incredible. It's almost as good as sex. Ooo, I wonder what it would be like to bungee jump *while* having sex. Probably not as good as it sounds. Where would your focus be? You're approaching orgasm and then you're in the free fall and bouncing all around, jamming and prodding each other, probably rather indelicately. And with my luck, I'd end up puking. Yes, not good at all."

Dhavin's frown deepened with her rapid speech. "What is this word, puking?"

"Ah, it's to *batkja*. When gravity loses and the contents of your stomach come out your mouth."

He sighed and shook his head. "I have so much to learn about this world. Intercourse on television, falling from the sky on purpose, this puking. I thought a year spent in a pod learning nothing but languages and politics would be enough."

"Do not worry, friend." She stroked his arm. "I'll show you the way."

Lucian emitted a sound that reminded her of a metal utensil caught in the gears of an industrial garbage disposal. He caught himself and threw her another glance. "Princess, please, sit back and put on your seatbelt."

"Why? I trust your skill behind the wheel."

"It's not *my* skill you need to worry about. Now please, sit back and put on your restraint. It's for your own good."

"I don't want to." It wasn't childish petulance that kept her from wearing the belt, but the vast distance between her seat and the occupants in the front. Even at only a few feet, the loss of their energy left her cold, as if she turned a furnace down to low.

He pulled over to the shoulder with a quick turn of the wheel. "I will not move us another inch until you put on your seatbelt."

Oh, now there it was. Trying to gain some of his control back, assert his authority was he?

She folded her arms. "Then I guess we'll be here awhile."

Dark-green gaze clashed with lavender in the rearview mirror and the air thickened. With each harsh breath the windows grew cloudy until the entire view became obscured.

In her peripheral vision she saw Dhavin look back and forth between them then heave a sigh. "Since we won't be leaving anytime soon, I'll be searching for a shrub." He opened his door and disappeared from view.

A trickle of sweat beaded along her hairline and slid down the side of her face as the interior of the car grew more humid, yet she didn't do more than blink when it became absolutely necessary. Lucian's nostrils flared in tiny pulses and a muscle along his jaw twitched.

Her thighs bunched with the urge to shift in her seat as heat pulsed in her groin. Damn the man was sexy when he was being a hardass. His nostrils flared again as if he could scent her arousal. With a mental smile, she allowed a tendril of lust free to sweep along his emotional barrier, and wanted to giggle in delight when his left eye began to twitch.

That's right, Lucian, make me. What else would you like to make me do?

With myriad lascivious thoughts running through her mind, she swept the tip of her tongue along her lips and almost whimpered when his gaze followed the motion. His hands tightened on the steering wheel and his arms trembled, yet he didn't make a move.

Who knew that such a show of strength would hit her like a powerful aphrodisiac? Sure, she might have a streak of masochistic tendencies, but if she continued on like this, she might require therapy.

Dhavin returned several minutes later. "Ah, still at it. Look, Amaryllis, *lebshone*, please clip on your belt. I'm getting hungry and I want you to introduce me to the wonder that is chocolate. I promise we won't discuss anything exciting during the rest of the journey."

She glanced at the comforting hand he placed on her knee then back up at his brown eyes that implored her to play nice. "Fine."

Lucian swiped a hand over his face while muttering a few obscenities in several languages then put the car into gear the second her belt clicked into place.

Did she deserve his scorn? Maybe. But whenever he spoke to her in that superior tone of voice she wanted to do the exact opposite of what he said, no matter how stupid the action may be. The reaction was pure impulse, like his voice struck her bitch nerve and the words spewed out. When he pushed, she wanted to shove back with all her might. Childish for certain, but it was her primary response, and the last thing she wanted Lucian to think of her as was a child. She would behave.

For now.

Silence stretched with each passing mile and her skin felt tight and constricting the longer she sat still. Her fingers rubbed along the edge of her suede jacket, worrying the knap in one direction then working it the other way.

Separated again because of her station. Alone with her royalty. No longer a person, she was precious cargo, relegated to the back and away from the "help". Why did everyone think that if you wore the mantle of princess, you wanted to be left alone? Too royal to consort with such mundane concepts as friendships, and too emotional to be given responsibilities in the court.

A humorless chuckle lodged in her throat. When she wanted to be left alone, she was dragged into society, and when she wanted to be involved, she was shunned. Thus continued the cycle of her former existence.

Several more miles passed with nothing but the whirl of tires racing across the asphalt and an occasional murmur between the two men. How she longed to be part of their conversation, no matter how brief and unimportant it might be.

She leaned forward and the strap across her chest bit into her breasts. She pulled it loose and tried again. "How long until we reach Pinetree?" she shouted.

"Cedar," Lucian replied. "The town's name is Cedar. And about thirty minutes."

"And what do you do in Cedar?" More importantly who do you do, she really wanted to know.

"Kristos and I work for a man named Harlan Kilsgaard. He found us when we crashed landed and took us in, gave us his name and a background. He owns a shop that sells outdoor sporting equipment and runs tours down the river."

That brought her up straighter in her seat. "Like white-water rafting? Really? Take me, please? That sounds like fantastic fun."

"No."

"Why not?"

"Because this is not a vacation."

"What are you expecting me to do, sit on my arse all day?"

"Yes."

"Completely unacceptable. If you won't take me, I'll ask Kristos."

"He will be otherwise occupied."

"Not all of the time, or he can take me after this Bale business is taken care of."

An unintelligible mutter passed from his lips. She was about to ask him to repeat himself when he changed the subject. "The colonists think Kristos and I are Harlan's nephews from Norway. You two will be cousins who are visiting us."

"Kissing cousins?" she asked.

In the review mirror she saw Lucian's lips tighten for a second before a brief grin emerged and he gave his head a little shake. That tiny crack in his venerable armor of irritation sent a shivery thrill to her tummy and she wanted to make him do it again.

His eyes met hers in the mirror. "This may be an impossible request, but can you try to remain inconspicuous?"

"Me? Why I practically fade into the wallpaper."

He let loose a snort of laughter. "All you have to do is walk into a room and you attract attention, that I am not oblivious to, but if you can turn down your brightness, it will make protecting you easier."

Was that a compliment? "I make no promises, but I can try to not be so spectacular."

Those green eyes of his sparkled and his suppressed laughter tickled her exposed skin. "That is all I ask, Your Highness."

"Shall I wear a shroud and communicate solely by hand signals?"

"Perfect." He looked at her again in the mirror and shocked her with a wink. His smile widened when she laughed with her surprise.

Soon they came upon a sign that read *Cedar. Population 3552.* An anxiety of a different sort fluttered in her stomach and had her fingers clutching the hem of her jacket.

Since landing on Earth, she spent almost all of her time in the city. Occasionally one of her friends whisked her out on a weekend away to another metropolis, but she never had the desire to explore Little Town, USA. From what she had heard, the smaller the colony, the smaller the mind, and she hated when anyone was discouraged from following their heart's desires.

What would Cedar's residents think of her, she wondered, because she had no intention of remaining shut away the entire three days. Isolation was as claustrophobic as a strait-jacket and compelled her to do irrational things. Besides, if she stayed hidden, how would she ever learn more information about her new favorite obsession?

Hundred-foot pine trees gave way to tiny ranch-style houses and picket-fence-lined roads. The thinner the trees grew, the more difficult she found it to breathe. Why she wanted the approval of absolute strangers was beyond her. She had thought that need to be accepted was long gone, yet a single car ride brought a magnifying mirror up to the lie she had been telling herself the last few years.

They rounded a bend and she spotted a dark wooden house with the words Cedar Sports and Marine emblazoned across the roofline in big red letters. As they approached, Kristos appeared on the deck accompanied by an older man and a woman dressed in a tan uniform. The clothes may have been designed for a man, but on her they emphasized the power of her femininity, and her innate sexuality only added to her air of authority.

Envy curled around Amaryllis in a cloyingly bitter ache. She didn't need her powers of empathy to know Kristos and his wife had found their perfect match in each other that went beyond their shared hair and eye color. Their contentment smashed through the glass of the car window and slammed Amaryllis in the chest.

What would it be like to have someone know you so intimately, feel your every fear and desire and act upon them accordingly? The trust one would have to place in the other was one of the most frightening things imaginable. And yet she still had those girlish dreams to find someone like that for herself.

Maybe in another lifetime.

Under the layer of the mates' solidarity, Amaryllis picked up the prickly sensation of apprehension, which made her smile. Whatever did they have to be nervous about? She was the stranger intruding upon their world. If anything, they should feel put out by the inconvenience.

Well, there was no need for all of them to be on edge. What was the phrase? Yes, she'd take the bull by the balls and make everyone happy.

Before Lucian brought the vehicle to a full stop, Amaryllis jumped out and raced up the porch steps.

"Kristosllanos," she shouted and threw her arms around his shoulders for a tight hug. She pulled back to place a kiss on each cheek then laid her hands on either side of his lean face. "It is so good to see you. Congratulations on your bonding. My mother would have been so happy for you. She always thought of you as more of a son than guard. You know she would have had the biggest, most lavish wedding gift created for you and be begging you to produce babies for her to spoil."

"Thank you, Your Highness." The words came out in a low, harsh whisper and his eyes filled with tears. His chest expanded as if an invisible heaviness rose from his body and he was able to breathe with ease for the first time in a long while.

A matching sting blurred her own vision. To know he held on to the guilt for so long angered her as much as it did cement her affection for this fine warrior.

It should not have surprised her that no one held Kristos more accountable for his unwitting role in her mother's death than Kristos. She had been en route to Earth when she had read the news reports in her spacecraft. The accounts she had heard about his punishment and subsequent banishment had broken her heart, for Queen Moira had loved her guard and would have never wanted him hurt by the actions she had taken. The blame lay elsewhere, and she hoped that Kristos would finally be able to put the past behind him.

Hmm, it seemed both brothers still had a lot of healing to do.

His Adam's apple bobbed twice, then he managed a watery smile and placed a kiss onto each of her palms. "It is good to see you too. If I had known you were so close, I would have come to see you."

She looked over her shoulder to see Lucian with his ever-present scowl and shot him a tight smile. "Yes, I've heard my location was a well-guarded secret. But enough about that, please, I want to meet your wife."

"Of course." He drew his woman forward. "Your Highness, may I present to you my wife, Brett. *Alskata*, this is Her Royal Highness, the Princess Amaryllis Moira Mathea Rosenorn."

"It's a pleasure to meet you, Your Highness." Brett dipped into an awkward bow-curtsy posture.

"Please, call me Amaryllis, for I hope you and I will become great friends." She clasped Brett's face between her hands and bestowed a kiss of friendship on each cheek. "I thank you for providing me shelter during this rather unwelcome situation. I only wish we could have met under different circumstances."

"Locking up bad guys is my calling. I'm happy to provide whatever assistance I can."

"As long as you're kept out of Bale's reach," Kristos added.

The flash of defiance that sparked in Brett's jade-green eyes tickled Amaryllis. "We shall see, sweetie."

"I see you have experienced the joys of being mated to a *Llanos*." Amaryllis laughed and turned to the man standing off to the side. "You must be Harlan. I've heard so much about you. It appears you are now my uncle too. I do hope I become your favorite niece." She kissed his whiskered cheek.

His peach skin turned a rosy red, and with his white beard, Harlan reminded her of the paintings of Santa Claus that decorated the city each winter. He tugged at the straps of his overalls and had to clear his throat before he said, "Welcome to my home, Ms. Amaryllis. I hope you enjoy your time here."

"I'm sure we'll have great fun."

"The house is on the other side of the store. Let's get you inside and settled in your room. It's not much, but you'll be comfortable, and Dhavin will be right next door to you."

"Your generosity is really all I require."

"Wait." Lucian stopped them before they crossed the threshold. "There's been a change of plans. The princess will stay with Kristos and Brett."

"Why?" Kristos asked. "Not that we wouldn't love to have you, Your Highness, but I thought she was staying here where Harlan and Dhavin can keep an eye on her while we patrol."

"I have recently come across some new information and I think it best she stay with you."

"What information?"

Lucian glanced briefly at his cousin. "Come with me and I'll fill you in. We won't be long. Dhavin, if you will join us."

"Why do they do that?" Brett muttered as she glared at their retreating backs with her hands planted on her hips. "Like I'm not going to find out what they're talking about anyway."

"Lucian probably thinks he's protecting my modesty. You see, he learned this morning that Dhavin and I have...a history together."

Harlan choked on a breath of air as Brett's eyebrows shot up to her hairline. "Really?" she drew out in long syllables.

"Are you two still an item?"

"No, but we are good friends. However, the general does not like his guards being friendly with the royals, and he forgets that my personal business is just that, mine."

"I was wondering why he was looking like something crawled up his ass and twisted his intestines. Not that he's usually a laid-back kind of guy, but he does seem more intense than normal. Even for a *Llanos*."

Amaryllis tossed her head back and laughed from her belly. Brett joined her and Amaryllis felt an instant kinship form between the two of them. "So true. No wonder you are in a position of power. You are as observant as you are intelligent and beautiful."

Brett bit her lip as a flush of pink stained her cheeks. "I think that's one of the nicest compliments I've ever received. Thank you."

"Rubbish," Harlan interjected. "We say nice things to her all the time, she just has a hard time believing it." He patted Brett on the shoulder then offered his arm to Amaryllis. "While the young'uns are blustering about, why don't I take you on a little tour of the place?"

"I would love that."

The interior of the store was much larger than it appeared from the outside. Amaryllis had never seen so many guns lining one wall since her time spent in the armory back home. On the opposite wall hung the rifle's more peaceful cousins, the fishing rods, separated by racks of raincoats and shiny hip-waders, and shelves stocked with camping gear she never imagined existed. Did humans really enjoy spending their time off out in the woods so much?

When Harlan offered her a cup of coffee, she declined with a polite smile. If the acrid stench of burnt caffeine hadn't warned her, Brett's brief, but violent, shake of the head confirmed her decision.

Outside orange and red kayaks were lined up like soldiers ready to depart on their next mission and an oversized raft rested on the bank of the river, beckoning her to climb in and play in the rapids.

"That looks like such fun. Do you go often?" she asked Harlan.

"No, my rafting days are long over, so I leave it to the boys."

"And you miss it."

"I do." A wicked light entered his eyes. "But I'm not without a bit of adventure now and again." He waggled his brows and checked over his shoulder before looking at them as if he were about to impart a great secret. "Follow me."

Behind the store was a large shed that housed more rafting and kayaking equipment. In the corner sat six motorbikes, each with a helmet hanging off a handlebar.

"Harlan," Brett exclaimed. "You still ride?"

"On occasion, when the weather's good and no one's around to tell me I'm too old to be on one of these things. But I do enjoy a good ride through the woods now and again."

"Why so many?" Amaryllis trailed a finger over a worn seat and noticed a number spray painted on the tank. "You rent them out?"

"Sure do. During the tourist season."

"I don't fault you for the impulse, Harlan. I love to ride too. Once it's in your blood, the calling never leaves."

"You ride bikes, Princess?" Brett appeared more stunned by that than at Harlan's declaration.

"It's such a rush. I have two Harleys and a Triumph. That one is my favorite. I've never been on a dirt bike before."

"You should go while you're here. There's a nice little path that follows the river that's great for beginners."

Amaryllis looked out onto the parking lot where the three men were involved in a heated conversation. The brothers were talking at the same time while Dhavin stared them down with his arms crossed and the muscles of his biceps flexing with restrained action.

She looked up at Harlan and batted her lashes. "Is the path long?"

"Fifteen minutes, unless you deviate to the path that heads toward the falls. That one takes about an hour."

"You know, I would love to see more of Cedar's countryside, and since the men are still occupied, I think there is no better time than the present."

Brett glanced out to the roosters clucking like a bunch of hens and released a wide smile. "I like the red one."

Amaryllis smiled back. "I knew we were going to be great

friends. I like the red one too."

✦ ✦ ✦

"LUCIAN, THERE IS no reason to change the plan. Amaryllis will be fine here with me."

Dhavin was going to have to stop linking himself and the princess together or else the vein pounding in Lucian's forehead was going to explode.

"What happened?" his brother asked. "Why the change?"

Lucian glanced up at the three spectators watching them from the porch and switched to their native language. "Dhavin has violated the princess, and I think it best to keep them separated."

"What?"

"We had sex, and it was mutual. I did not violate her."

Kristos rounded on his cousin. "You touched the princess?"

"She needed me!"

"That's grounds for execution!"

"Enough," Lucian roared. "Regardless of your past, the truth of the matter is she has you wrapped around her delicate little finger. I believe your focus has been compromised."

Dhavin let loose with a bark of laughter. "This from the man who wants to fuck her so badly, I can taste your lust for her."

To hear his deepest shame blurted out with such crudeness smacked him like a metal gauntlet across the cheek. "That is not true."

Amaryllis let go with a peal of laughter that brought all of their heads around. The low, flirty notes gripped him by the balls and shot down his shaft, as if to punish him for spouting such a blatant lie.

"What are you really worried about, Lucian? Do you think that in the middle of the night Amaryllis is going to remember the pleasure she found in my arms and seek me out? That it will be me holding her by her silken hair while I feed her my cock? She likes it hard and rough, and I know just how to satisfy her."

Only Kristos' strong arm banded across his chest kept Lucian from taking his cousin to the gravel and striking a killing blow. "Don't you speak of her in such a vulgar manner."

"She likes it vulgar."

"Dhavin," Kristos shouted. "Do you want to die?"

"You didn't have to spend the entire day trapped between the two of them, snipping and bitching at each other when all they wanted was to strip naked and fuck. The tension was unbearable. I was tempted to leave them in the car all day until they finally jumped each other so we could all move on. Perhaps now you will get over yourself, Lucian, and go to her."

Lucian clamped his teeth together. Damn, he thought he had controlled his emotions better. Nonetheless, he would not give in to the temptation.

"If you continue to speak of the princess with such disrespect, I will gut you where you stand."

Dhavin rolled his eyes at the threat. "I speak the truth. Do not worry about me keeping my focus. I will lay down my life to protect Amaryllis, as I have since the day I made my oath to the House of Rosenorn."

"And what of you, Lucian?"

He looked at his brother as if he'd grown a second head. "I will protect her 'til my last breath. I am *Llanos*. Never question that."

"I mean, do you desire her for your own?"

With every beat of his hearts, but admitting that was not a good idea at this time. Possibly never.

"My feelings for the princess are irrelevant. It is my honor to protect her and protect her I will."

The two men shared a look that said they weren't buying his bullshit.

"What is wrong with you wanting her, Lucian?" Dhavin asked. "She's a beautiful woman. Vibrant. Passionate. And she desires you too. What is stopping you?"

Dhavin was the devil sitting on his shoulder, seducing him with what he shouldn't covet, yet craved more than anything he ever wanted. Only his honor kept him from crossing the line he had spent his entire life defending.

"I am her servant and always will be. I will stand by her bed, but never warm it."

His cousin shook his head. "You are a fool."

Then a fool he shall be.

The high-pitched wail of an engine rent the air. Lucian

turned toward the sound in time to see a streak of red with silver hair trailing behind like a flag disappear into the tree line.

"Harlan! What have you done?"

The older man shrugged. "She has experience. Besides, she's only going on the short trail. She'll be back in a minute."

"Or she could be killed."

Without a second thought, Lucian was off, racing after the trail of dust and exhaust that snaked around giant tree trunks, ferns and blackberry bushes.

"Amaryllis!" he shouted with all the force he could muster.

His lungs ached and his thighs burned as he ran faster than any human on the planet. She maintained just out of his reach, which only spoke of the dangerous speed she used over the rough terrain.

The turnabout came up and she blew past it, heading deeper into the woods and following the lip of the gorge. Rocks shot out from under the rear tire, skittering over the edge and into the rushing Cedar River a hundred feet below.

"Amaryllis! Halt! I command you!" he forced out from a throat tight with fear.

Her leather-booted foot hit the ground as she muscled the bike into a controlled spin. Dust billowed around her as she whipped off her helmet and shook out her hair in a cloud of silver.

"What are you doing?" she asked. The innocence of her query jabbed him like a hot poker to the belly.

"What—what am—" He bent double, his hands braced on his shaky knees as he fought for breath. "You. You are insane. Do you realize how far you've traveled?"

"Nobody asked you to chase after me."

"Apparently I'm the only one who cares for your safety."

"Why?"

"What?"

She brought her leg over the body of the bike and stood tall before him. "Why do you care so much about my safety?"

"It is my duty."

"Duty?" An invisible wall came up between them so fast it slammed against his chest. "Is that all? Is that what I am, Lucian? A job? When will you get it through that thick skull of yours that we are no longer in court? You are not my guard. You never were. I don't need you to take care of me."

"But you do need me. You have no concept of the evil out to kill you. You are defenseless, and if you continue to disregard my knowledge and expertise, you might as well serve him your head on a platter."

"I pity you, General. You think too much with your head, and not with your hearts."

The barrier around her emotions was strong, but even so, a thread of hurt snaked out and tugged at the hearts she claimed he didn't have. "Amaryllis."

She stopped his speech with an imperious raise of her hand. "I officially relieve you of your *duty*."

And with that, she took a step back, right off the edge of the cliff.

Chapter Five

L UCIAN STOOD ROOTED to the ground, his mind unable to comprehend the unbelievable sight. It was absolutely inconceivable. One moment the princess was looking at him with hurt and disappointment in her wide eyes and the next, she was gone. The tips of her silver hair the last thing he saw after she stepped off the cliff.

By the Gods. She stepped off the cliff!

The realization propelled him into action and he ran to the edge and peered down to the rushing river. Confusion clouded his vision. There was no sign of her, no body, no hint of her red coat, nothing. Was she already swept away by the fast current?

Without hesitation, he leapt off the edge and landed gracefully on the rocky bank and began to run downstream. "Amaryllis!"

"Yes?"

He spun around at the sound of her voice and his knees buckled. She sat on a large boulder, one leg crossed over the other, her little foot bouncing in a rhythm that matched the drumming of her fingers.

"I think, General, you've forgotten that I too went through

the same change you boys did, and I'm stronger and faster than any human on Earth. I'm not the delicate flower you insist on treating me like."

Relief sapped his strength and he nearly collapsed at her feet to bury his head in her lap. He wanted to feel her alive and warm in his arms, but he clung to his anger instead of giving in to the compulsion.

"Why do you insist on playing these childish games? What have I ever done to you to warrant such behavior?"

She raised an incredulous brow. "You've done nothing but treat me like an imbecile and like I have no feelings. You order me around as if I haven't the logic to understand what is going on. Did I not do what you asked as soon as you brought me proof of Bale? I'm an experienced rider and I asked Harlan for the easiest trail because the terrain is unfamiliar. The question isn't what have you done to me, but what have I done to you to make you think I am incapable of knowing anything?"

He opened his mouth to unleash the lengthy list, then realized that in actuality, he had nothing. Amaryllis was a royal and he her protector. As such, his position granted him absolute rule over one thing, her well-being, and it was a responsibility he'd give his life to fulfill.

Amaryllis was like an epic song that moved through your entire body, bringing you to tears before releasing you back to your humdrum existence. At her club he witnessed firsthand how her patrons watched her with an admiration won by action and not false words. To have her spirit silenced was unacceptable and she needed to be protected by any means necessary, which was why he fought with her over her independence.

Men showed courage with action and brawn. Amaryllis showed hers with leading by example. Lucian marveled at her strength, but by the same token it scared the shit out of him. That type of courage was bred to the bone. A part of her DNA that was unchangeable. Perhaps he had been arrogant to believe she would accept his command without a whimper, that he could set aside all emotion and treat her like another mission, just as she accused. However, his dominance was part of *his* DNA and unchangeable as well.

Continuously butting heads was not going to keep her safe. He needed her trust more than he needed to be right, and he had no one but himself to blame for the wall standing between them.

"I will not apologize for my tactics for keeping you safe, however I am sorry if my methods have given you the impression that I think you are weak, because I don't," he admitted. "In fact, I think you are one of the bravest people I have ever known."

Surprise widened her eyes. "That's not true! You think I'm a childish harlot."

The vehemence behind her words wounded him like a hot lash across his chest. "I never said that."

"You thought it. I felt it."

"I've never, Amaryllis. Not once." Did she really believe he thought so little of her? He gestured to the rock she sat upon. "May I?"

A delicate frown touched her brow as her lavender gaze raked him from head to toe. He waited patiently with his spine straight and shoulders back as he withstood her inspection. Finally she granted him a slight nod. "You may."

Yet she didn't slide over to create more room for his larger frame. Their arms and hips pressed together and her heat seeped to his bones that he hadn't realized were so cold.

He swallowed hard, resisting the urge to press closer. "When the time came for you to be evacuated from the palace, you were terrified. Even with my barriers in place, I could still taste your fear. Your father and I were not positive we were sending you to a better place and all you were armed with was your intelligence and a box of crown jewels. I was half tempted to pull you from the craft and find some other way to keep you from the revolutionaries. But despite the turmoil you emoted, on the outside, you were so composed, so calm and regal. Your strength and courage were breathtaking."

She shrugged. "What was I supposed to do? Fall to the floor and beg to stay? I was leaving my home forever. The least I could do was maintain my dignity."

"Your exile was never meant to be permanent, Your Highness. As soon as it was safe, you would have been called home."

"And look how well that plan worked." In light of her sarcasm, a smile curved her lips. "It's all right, General. I am so much happier here than I ever was on Skandavia. I've taken lemons and made them into a delicious lemon-vodka martini rimmed with sugar."

"Yes, you most certainly have."

She was much like Kristos in that regard. When they had arrived on Earth, his brother had thrown himself into their new reality, seeking joy in the everyday to overcome the pain of the past. But Lucian was always aware that Kristos' failure was never far from his thoughts and colored his every action. At least that had always been the case before, perhaps now that demon was finally slayed, thanks to Amaryllis.

"Thank you for what you said to Kristos. I don't think you know just how much he needed to hear those words."

"I spoke the truth. My mother had committed herself to her people. Nothing would sway her from doing what she believed was right. The only person to blame for my mother's death is Hamerkind. It was wrong of my father to lay the blame on you and Kristos."

"I would have too. His bonded mate had been murdered, his family gone—"

"Then place blame on the man who was really at fault. It was my father's choice to not listen to his people and seek peace in the first place. You and your brother were many of the causalities of his stubbornness. His arrogance cost too many lives."

"He cared for his people."

"But he cared about his image more." She picked up a

stone lying near her feet and skipped it to the other side of the riverbank with a soft snick of her wrist. "We can't dwell on the misery, Lucian. It helps no one. Let's focus on the good. Kristos found his happiness. Would that have happened had he remained on Skandavia?"

"Probably not."

"And you. Are you happy, Lucian?"

A reply came readily to his lips, but the earnest light in her eyes gave him pause. If there was anyone who might understand his lack of connection to his new life, perhaps it was the princess.

"I should be. I'm alive." He gestured to the craggy green hills and rushing river with the sunlight sparkling along its rippled edges. "I live amongst this beauty. I have my family close. Aren't I supposed to be happy?"

"But you don't have a purpose."

He looked at her sharply, surprised that she arrowed with deadly accuracy to the heart of his discontent. "I used to command hundreds of men. Every second of my day was scheduled. I was part of something great that held true meaning. Now I spend hours balancing ledgers and debating with retirees the best weight of line to use bass fishing. It doesn't compare."

"Haven't you traveled? Explored the world?"

"No. Not really. The only time I've left Cedar was to check on you."

A delighted smile curled her lips. "Lucian, I want you to

make me a promise."

The request intrigued him more than he wanted.

"When this Bale situation is over, I want you to take a trip. Leave Cedar. Leave the state. Go away and experience other cultures. Taste life. Find your purpose. Promise me."

Lucian gazed into her fathomless lavender eyes, easily picturing a future where he walked the streets of London, climbed the steppes of the Andes or took in a play in New York. And in each vision, Amaryllis was at his side.

"I promise."

Her smile softened, drawing his gaze to the soft pad of her lips. Like a reed in a breeze he swayed, drawing closer, so close he scented the sugary drink consumed during their journey on her breath. Would her kiss taste as sweet?

She tilted her head to the right, her lips parting as she swayed closer. "Lucian," she mouthed against his lips.

"Princess," he whispered.

Princess.

He jerked away from her so quickly, he lost his balance and fell off the rock. His arms flailed as he landed in the gravel with a hard grunt.

"Lucian," Amaryllis shouted. "Are you all right?"

"I'm fine." He jumped to his feet as if nothing was amiss. "It's, um, it's getting late. We should head back."

That shrewd look narrowed her eyes again. The look that made him feel naked and exposed.

With a nod she stood and brushed the seat of her pants.

"As you wish, General. Race you to the top."

Her saucy wink was the last he saw before she disappeared in a streak of red suede and silver hair. When he finally caught sight of her, she was scaling the side of the cliff as naturally as a spider monkey. A melodic trill of laughter drifted from above, spurring him to action.

He followed, but at a slower pace, needing the distance to pull his mind from the images inspired by those luscious lips. Not more than an hour before he chastised Dhavin for his inappropriate relationship with the princess and now he was entertaining the very same thoughts. When the king had stripped him of everything he held dear, the only thing Lucian had been able to cling to was his honor. To fall to a weakness of the flesh would be a disgrace to that sacrifice. For the good of all, he must not succumb to such temptations.

"It took you long enough," Amaryllis said when he crested the top. "Perhaps this forced retirement has made you soft."

Soft? If she only knew.

Lucian strode toward the bike, resolutely ignoring the ache in his cock, and lifted it by the frame. "Come on. If we hurry, we can make it back before sunset."

"What are you doing? Put that down." She shook her head and strapped on the helmet. "We'll ride back."

"Ride back? I don't know how to ride that thing."

"Aren't you the same man who was the youngest champion of the Valhad Run with a speeder you built yourself that was faster and less sturdy than this cycle?"

"Yes, but that—"

"No. No lame excuses about how that was different. If you want me to return with you, you'll get your butt on that seat. Now."

"You're going to make this difficult for me, aren't you?"

"I can be rather sweet when I get my way."

"Your Highness, I don't want to endanger you."

"That's why I'm wearing the helmet. Come on, Lucian. What are you so afraid of?"

Dropping dead from blood loss to the head when you plaster that lush body against my back.

She'd do it too. Torturing him seemed to be her favorite pastime and there was no doubt she wouldn't pass up a prime opportunity to twist him into knots.

Heavens light, when had he become such a coward that the mere thought of being in close contact with a female made his knees knock? *Llanos* up, man.

With a tight smile Lucian strode to the bike and swung his leg over the seat. Once he was settled, Amaryllis pointed out all the features and related them to how a speeder worked back home. A good kick with his boot brought the machine to life, pulsing and thrumming between his thighs in a teeth-gritting tease. He choked back a moan when Amaryllis settled behind him, wiggling her shoulders so her breasts rubbed enticingly against his spine.

They were going to die. His head was going to explode and he was going to steer them right into a tree.

"Ready when you are, General," she shouted over the ping of the motor.

He released the throttle and the little bike took off like a shot. Her delighted laughter floated in the air as she wrapped her arms around his waist. As he dodged trees and shrubs, her hands wandered over his stomach. She traced the line of his tight abdominals with her fingertips, followed by the rasp of her nails. With the v-6 buzzing against his sac, his cock hardened, trapped in the stranglehold of his jeans. Sweat dripped into his eyes and he had to shake his head to bring his focus off the hands caressing lower and lower and onto the twisting trail ahead of them.

The wandering hands were bad enough, but combined with the vibration of her emotions, it was absolute torture. By the Gods, she was as aroused as he. He swore he scented the heady musk of her arousal over the scent of pine and diesel fuel. Her hips swiveled in the seat and a hot, pulsing sensation wrapped around him, dragging him further into her spell.

No, no, no! His hands tightened on the grips, refusing to turn them deeper into the woods to find a shaded area where he could give her the ride she was begging for.

The tips of her curious fingers edged under the waistband of his jeans.

Satan's foul ball sac! The woman didn't play fair.

He cranked the accelerator, blowing them both back in their seats. Amaryllis shrieked and clutched him tighter. Her thighs gripped his hips and her touch changed from sexual to self-preservation.

A hill came upon them he knew he should slow for, yet he gunned the motor, launching them over a jump. The frame of the bike bounced and shuddered when they hit ground, but it was worth it to hear Amaryllis laugh with unadulterated joy. He took another a jump, then another, basking in the bubbles that her laughter created over his skin. Such joy was impossible to ignore and he laughed with her, truly laughed for the first time since he became the head of the guard.

The sports shop appeared before he was ready for the ride to end. He drove them into the garage and cut the motor.

"That was fantastic," Amaryllis crowed as she jumped off the back. She removed the helmet and shook out her hair. "Say it. I want to hear the words."

He took his time rising. "That was fun," he admitted with a deep sigh.

With a rousing whoop, she raised her hands in the air and danced in a circle. When she faced him again, she laid her hand against his cheek, her thumb brushed along his lower lip.

"You're a handsome man when you smile."

He didn't move. Couldn't move, or he'd be on her, pulling her close for that kiss they both wanted.

The warmth of her fingers lasted long after she pulled away.

"I'll see you inside." She turned on her heel and swished away.

He lost count of the number of times she walked away

from him that day. But this time he reached out to pull her back. He dropped his outstretched hand and made sure every piece of equipment was where it belonged before returning to his post at her side.

✦   ✦   ✦

"BY THE GODS, Betty Sue. This chocolate cream pie is delicious. It's so luscious, I want to slather it all over my skin." Amaryllis brought her plate up to her face to capture the last few crumbs on her tongue.

Betty Sue beamed a gigantic smile and twirled the cherry earrings dangling from her lobes. "I can't believe Amaryllis Rosenorn is sitting in my diner, loving my food. Last year, for my birthday, my husband surprised me with dinner at your restaurant. It was the best meal I ever ate, and the environment was so romantic. Let me tell you, the mister was rewarded quite well for that treat." She waggled her finely arched brows.

Amaryllis laughed. "The next time you come to the city, you will dine again at my restaurant and I will not only seat you at the best table, but I will have the chef prepare you a special menu featuring his favorite dishes."

"Really? Oh that will be wonderful. This day is just getting better and better. Now I'm friends with a famous person."

"I wouldn't say I'm famous. However, some may say I am infamous."

"And that's the best type of famous to be," Brett piped from the next barstool over.

Amaryllis watched as the blonde flicked her tongue between each tine of her fork to collect every speck of cream. "Oh now I know why Kristos loves you so."

A red flushed streaked across her cheeks. "You are so bad."

"So I've been told."

"You know, I noticed you and Lucian seemed to have put aside your differences last night."

"He agreed to stop being so bossy, and I agreed to stop pushing his buttons. Most of the time."

"That's too bad. I like seeing Lucian flustered." She shrugged a deceptively casual shoulder. "Hey, have you thought about staying in town a few days longer? You haven't really had a chance to explore the countryside."

"You're plotting something, Sheriff. I can feel it like little feet marching down my spine."

She stuck out her tongue. "I hate when you guys do that. Let me keep my emotions to myself."

"Then learn how to keep them to yourself. Especially if you're making devious plans about Lucian and me."

"It's just that I find you two very entertaining when you're together. You challenge him and I don't think he's had that in a really long time. Besides, the boys think they're the shit and I have my hands full with Kristos being the protective warrior. You can work on relaxing Lucian. Around you he seems more...human."

The women held each other's gazes for a moment before they burst out in peals of laughter.

"Did I hear you can make Lucian flustered?" Betty Sue topped off their mugs of coffee. "I'd pay to see that. He is one yummy man. So strong and mysterious. But he's also so somber. You know, I don't think I've ever seen him laugh, really laugh, like you two have been doing all afternoon. It's like he has this shell around him that no one can break through, and believe me, honey, almost every single woman in this town has tried."

Really? Amaryllis was intrigued. "There must have been at least one woman who's captured his interest."

Both Betty Sue and Brett wore identical frowns as they each looked into the distance. Finally Brett shook her head while Betty Sue answered, "Nope, not really."

No wonder Lucian was as tense as a tightrope. She lifted her cup in a toast. "Then it's a good thing I'm in town. Sounds like the poor man needs to release some steam. Ah—"

A sharp, pain shot down Amaryllis' neck to her hand. The mug dropped from her grip to smash against the countertop.

"Amaryllis?" Brett got to her feet as frantic screaming came from the street outside.

"There's a child in danger." She jumped from her seat and raced to the diner's front window.

Bright-orange flames licked the underside of the overhang of a nearby gas station. The source of the fire was a sedan. The petrol hose was still in the tank, feeding the flames consuming pump and car. A man ran around the vehicle, his face stretched with horror as he approached the smoking door handle then sprang back when the heat became too much to bear.

Brett shot out of the diner and began barking orders into her police radio. "Unit one to base. I need fire units to the gas station on Maple and Main. Car is engulfed in flames and there may be a child trapped inside."

Amaryllis followed, joined by what seemed like the entire town.

"I forgot," the man yelled at Brett as she ran full speed toward him. "I was smoking and forgot. Mikey. Mikey's inside."

A squad car pulled up, and then another and another. While the officers were busy keeping the gathering crowd at bay and devising a plan for rescue, little Mikey cried and shrieked with fear. His terror reached across the distance and squeezed Amaryllis around the throat. Tears streamed down her face as she tried to use her powers to send some comfort to the boy. How was he to understand that the more he panicked, the faster he used up all the available oxygen in the car? Perhaps she was wishing for the impossible, but what else could she do? Race in and pull him from the vehicle?

Wait. Why couldn't she? She had the strength, she had the speed. All she needed was a way to slip in unseen. There were only a hundred, maybe two hundred, potential witnesses clustered on the sidewalk, all gaping with wide eyes and cellphones glued to the rescue efforts of the police.

Right. No problem.

"My boy! Please, my boy!"

No. She could do this. Had to do this. A life, maybe more, was at stake.

She edged her way to the back of the crowd and skirted around to where she had a direct line to the passenger door. Her muscles tensed to run when another cry rang out.

"It's him! It's him!"

Shouts of "the Chameleon" grew louder and more fevered as the crowd pointed in the distance. A streak of black and gray raced past the police barricade and her mouth dropped open as the incredible sight unfolded before her.

By. The. Gods.

This was a hallucination. It had to be. She blinked hard once, then again, but the image remained the same.

The newcomer wore the royal armor of a Skandavian guard. His torso shimmered with the reflection of the flames, making the outline of his body disappear into the environment. The black cowl covering his head may have concealed his identity, but Amaryllis recognized those firm lips and that cleft chin in an instant.

Lucian.

With nary a pause he reached out and grasped the handle of the car door, tearing it free from the hinges and tossing it aside as if it weighed no more than a paper plate.

Ignoring the flames, he reached inside and wrenched the toddler from the wreckage, car seat and all. His image blurred again as he raced to the waiting paramedics and delivered his precious cargo. The child was in safe hands, but the Chameleon wasn't finished yet. He traced inside the store and returned with two fire extinguishers and went to work on the worst of the blaze.

Spectators jostled around Amaryllis, angling for the best view of the hero in action. She ducked and weaved, searching for the perfect view herself. Damn her small stature, she cursed as she stepped back and jumped, clearing four feet of air to see over the heads of the humans blocking her view.

The blare of sirens heralded the arrival of the fire department. With most of the flames doused, Lucian nodded to the firemen then ran back in the direction he had come from.

Amaryllis was torn with the desire to chase after him and grill him for answers and staying to assist however she could.

Brett jogged up to her side. "Amaryllis, I'm gonna be awhile. Let me get one of my men to take you home."

"I can make it back myself. It looks like you could use all the help you can get."

She snorted. "I can spare one to take you home. Reutgers," she shouted, drawing the attention of a young deputy. "I need you to take my friend here to my house and stay with her until Kristos or one of the other Kilsgaards meet you there."

"Brett, I don't need a babysitter."

"And I don't need three overprotective men jumping on my ass," she snapped, then closed her eyes on an inhale and laid her hand on Amaryllis' arm. "I'm sorry. Please don't think that I believe you incapable of taking care of yourself, but I'd be able to concentrate better if I knew you weren't alone."

"I understand. I'll be good."

Brett relaxed with a soft smile. "First chance we get, you and I are heading to the city to raise the kind of hell that will turn my husband's hair white. Promise?"

"It's a date. But before I go, would you like to briefly explain what it was I just saw?"

"Yeah, about that. Sorry, it'll take time to tell you properly. I will tell you, later though. I promise. Reutgers is one of my best deputies. He'll take care of you. Reutgers, this is my friend, Amaryllis. She's family to Kristos, and you know how he can get about the safety of his family. Treat her like gold."

"Yes ma'am." He turned toward Amaryllis and tilted his hat in greeting. "Ms. Amaryllis, may I escort you to my vehicle?"

"Oh my. Handsome and good manners. I'm impressed." She hooked her elbow with his and cupped her free hand around his biceps. "Please, lead the way. Do you have a first name, Deputy?"

A pink flush darkened his cheeks. "It's Rhett. But everyone calls me Reutgers."

Why was he embarrassed about his name? With his short military haircut and strong jaw, she thought it was quite fitting. "Mother a *Gone with the Wind* fan?"

"No. My grandmother was a Clark Gable fan. I think I would have preferred Clark over Rhett."

"I like it. Rhett's a very bold name, unusual and has great impact. It suits you."

The flush darkened. "Thank you, ma'am."

"Please, call me Amaryllis."

They arrived at his squad car where he opened the passenger door. "All right. That's an unusual name too. Very pretty. Like you."

She offered him a warm smile as she sat upon the seat. He closed the door and came around to slide behind the wheel. As he started the car and began the journey to Brett's house, she turned in her seat to give the officer her full attention. From the corner of his eye, his gaze slipped down to the generous amount of cleavage she sported. His hands tightened on the wheel before he snapped his focus back to the windshield and swallowed hard.

Never let it be said that she was opposed to using any means necessary to obtain what she wanted.

"So, Rhett," she began, "what happened back there? Who was that man in that crazy suit?"

"Oh that." His shoulders relaxed as if talking about a masked crusader was more preferable than being the object of her attention. "We all call him the Chameleon, because of the way his suit blends in with the surroundings. Whenever someone is in need, he appears out of nowhere, saves the day then disappears just as quick as he arrived."

"He's a vigilante?"

"Used to be, but Sheriff Briggs put an end to that right quick. You could say that he's more of a good Samaritan."

"And he's always in the suit?"

"Yep."

"And no one knows who he is?"

"That's right."

Seriously? How many men were crawling around Cedar who were six-and-a-half-feet tall with broad shoulders, a tapered waist and a mouth that begged to be softened with slow kisses? If there was more than one, she'd have to pack her bags and move out here permanently.

"How come I've never heard of this Chameleon? Why hasn't he been in the news?"

"The local paper ran a few stories on him, but I guess the idea is so crazy the bigger papers didn't pick up on it. Plus folks around here like the idea that the Chameleon belongs to the people of Cedar and want to keep it that way. Especially the ladies."

It was soft, but the bite of jealousy at the end of his sentence plucked at her awareness. "Popular, is he?"

"If it's not the Kilsgaard brothers they're panting after, then it's the Chameleon."

Yes, that would be quite a tough act to follow. "I don't know, Rhett. I'm sure some of them think rather dirty thoughts about you too."

His Adam's apple bobbed again. "I—I don't know about that."

"Why not? You're a handsome man with a strong jawline and deep, dark eyes. And women love a man in uniform. But do you know what the Chameleon has that you could have as well?"

"What?" He might have been playing it cool a moment ago, but once she dangled the carrot in front of him, his hunger for knowledge blew that façade to smithereens.

"Confidence. He strode right up to that fire without a moment's hesitation. Displays of courage are highly arousing."

He uttered a shaky laugh and readjusted his grip on the steering wheel.

"I saw that same confidence in you earlier when that fire was burning. You knew exactly how to control that crowd. The shy man I see before me now was not who you were then."

"That's different. In my job I know exactly what to do and say. It's different with women."

"Yet you're speaking to me just fine."

"That's because I know who your family is and that they'll hand me my ass on a platter if I act on any of the thoughts I've been having about you."

She laughed and relaxed back in her seat. "Then show that side to another woman. Be the man you are inside the uniform when you're out of uniform. Trust me, a smart woman will be honored to be on your arm."

"I'll try."

"No, Rhett. Do."

He flashed her a rueful grin. "Right. I will."

Satisfied that the message was received, she jerked in her seat with a gasp. "Oh, my phone." She withdrew her cellphone from her skirt pocket and looked at the blank screen. "Lucian sent me a text. He's home now. Could you be a dear and take me to his house instead of Brett's? Then you wouldn't have to wait for him to meet us there before returning to assist her."

"Sure thing, Ms. Amaryllis."

Lucky for her, Lucian's car was parked in the driveway, lending credence to her little lie. He was home all right, but she'd bet her last stiletto he didn't want her to know.

Reutgers moved to turn off the cruiser. "I'll see you inside."

"No need for that. You can watch me until I enter. How much trouble can I get into walking across the lawn?"

He smiled that crooked grin of his that made his eyes sparkle. "I have a feeling trouble follows wherever you go. That's why the sheriff asked me to watch you."

"Smart man. But I'll be fine, really." She leaned across the seat and bussed his cheek with a quick kiss. "Thank you for the ride, and remember, confidence, twenty-four-seven."

"You're welcome, Ms. Amaryllis. I hope to see you again."

"Me too, if you're not too busy beating away your admirers."

"Right." He laughed.

She hurried to the porch and offered a cheerful wave after she opened the front door with the key Dhavin had given her. As soon as she was inside the house, all frivolity faded and she stood in the foyer, reaching out with her powers. The only presence she detected was of one turbulent male whose emotions rolled from euphoric to despondent like an ocean tide during a storm. The sound of water rushing through the pipes brought her gaze up to the ceiling and an anticipatory grin curled her lips.

Lucian? In the shower?

"Perfect," she purred.

Slipping off her heels, she tiptoed up the stairs and down the hall to Lucian's room. The door was slightly ajar. How convenient.

The uneven splish-splash of the water as it sluiced off his body blew her focus to hell. Why was she here again? Right, question Lucian about this Chameleon character. To think, he had issues with her extracurricular activities. At least she wasn't purposefully placing herself in danger or exposing her powers. What exactly was his game, and why hadn't she thought of it first?

Splish. Splash. Splash-splash.

However…

A tremor shook her shoulders and her thighs became slick even as she struggled to temper her desire. There wasn't a living soul who knew what the next few moments would bring, but one thing was for certain, once Lucian stepped into this room, her life was never going to be the same. There was so much to be said, so much to do, change was inevitable. Adrenaline pumped through her veins, making the colors in the room appear sharper and her teeth chatter with anticipation.

The water shut off and Amaryllis drew a deep breath to slow the rapid beat of her hearts and block any telling emotions. So far Lucian gave no indication he knew she was close, and she wanted to keep it that way until the last possible moment.

Lucian strode from the bathroom, dripping wet with a towel draped over his head. Droplets of water clung as if loath to evaporate from his bronze skin. She couldn't blame them.

He lifted his head and jumped with a shout when he spotted her leaning against the dresser. He cupped the towel over his crotch, like that did anything to hide the erection that was rapidly growing by the second. "Ah! Amaryllis. I—what—I—"

"No." She waggled her finger at him. "No stammering. No stuttering. No hedging. No lies."

He swallowed hard. "What do you want?"

A tittering laugh welled from her throat. "Oh Lucian. I want so much. But first, you will tell me why I saw a man dressed in royal armor play superhero not more than thirty minutes ago."

His lips thinned and he swallowed again. "Let me get dressed first."

"Please don't cover up on my account." Her gaze lingered on the tented part of the towel.

"Amaryllis."

"No." She shook her head. "No. Talk. Now."

He chuffed out a frustrated breath and stroked his jaw. "It's nothing really. Kristos didn't like how Brett's job put her in danger. He tried to keep her out of harm's way and wore the armor while he was doing it. A while ago she was trapped underground during a rescue and he saved her, spawning the

Chameleon."

"And now you wear the mantle?"

"Not all the time. Kristos and I take turns to throw off suspicion. And the Chameleon only appears when there is a desperate need."

"Like earlier." She took one small step toward him, then another, approaching as one would an easily frightened animal. "You saved that child, Lucian. And who knows how many more by keeping that fire from spreading."

"I felt that child's pain from ten miles away. I had to do something."

"You're a hero, Lucian." She paused, mere millimeters away from his bare chest. "If I was that boy's mother, I would drop to my knees and offer you anything you wanted."

"A—" He cleared his throat. "Thank you is sufficient enough."

"Tell me about your last lover."

He blinked, clearly confused by the change in subject as the furrow in his brow deepened. "What?"

"Your last lover. Rumor has it you've gone a long time without female companionship, even though you weren't lacking for willing participants." She trailed her finger along the edge of her low-cut blouse. Her nipples tightened when his gaze followed the movement. "Why?"

"Your Highness," he began but she stopped him with a hand across his mouth.

"No lies. Why?" She moved her palm to lay it against his

jaw.

He licked at his lips. "I'm a warrior. A battle strategist. I don't know how to woo a woman. And human women are so…fragile."

"Physically or emotionally?"

A light flashed in his eyes and a tingle of awareness hummed in the air between them. "Both."

"I guess it's a good thing I'm not human or fragile."

"But you are. You'll deny it with your last breath, but I've hurt you when all I want to do is care for you."

"You do?"

"Of course."

He lifted his hand and barely grazed his finger along her jaw before dropping it at his side and making a fist.

"Touch me, Lucian."

"I can't. I shouldn't."

But he wanted to. Gods did he want to. Never before had she felt such a sense of want than she did looking up into his tortured eyes. His craving was bittersweet, like a fine Belgian chocolate sitting on the flat of your tongue. The flavor melting ever-so-slowly as you were forced to hold still when all you wanted was to chomp the decadent treat to bits and gobble it whole.

The promise of experiencing the full force of Lucian's passion made her stomach clench and her pussy gush. She leaned forward and scraped her teeth over his puckered nipple then used the tip of her tongue to follow a rivulet of water down his torso.

"I know you, Lucian. I know who you are. You don't need to hide from me. Never from me." Under her lips, his stomach quivered as tiny goose bumps erupted against her tongue.

"We shouldn't."

"No." She nipped at the taut skin around his navel and sank to her knees. "No."

A gentle tug of her fingers brought the towel to floor, freeing his engorged cock. She eagerly wrapped both hands around the shaft and licked the purple head. Now was not the time to think. If she allowed a moment of hesitation, he would run from her and the heat generating between them. A tragedy she'd never allow.

As she took the throbbing length into her mouth, a fiery bolt of desire raced from Lucian to explode across her senses as if she swallowed a mouthful of Pop Rocks.

Now this trait of the Skandavian male she missed dearly. The men of her homeland were all blessed with impressive cocks. A feature she had been fascinated by when she watched the troops during their wrestling drills. The heat of battle created a rush of adrenaline that resulted in erections that tented their thin fatigues and made her mouth water at the thought of slipping into their baths and tasting each one.

Lucian's cock was simply beautiful. Thick and long, he stretched her lips and pulsed against her tongue with a beat that grew more frenzied with every suckle of her throat. He smelled like a mountain breeze and tasted of feral need. He was wildness and restrained hunger, and she was eager to set it free.

A primal growl ripped past his lips as her cheeks hollowed and she stroked his tightening sac. His hands dove into her hair to hold her still for the frantic thrust of his hips. Through the veil of her lashes she watched the battle for dominance play across his features as his teeth clenched and his eyes threatened to close with the bliss that wrapped her in silken wings.

"Enough." He fisted the strands of hair and pulled, dragging her to a stand and claiming her lips in a bruising kiss. She shared his taste, tangling her tongue with his and daring him to lose control.

She allowed her hunger free rein to snake around them, driving the need higher. Lucian responded by meeting that desire with a force of his own that stripped her of all civility. The fabric of her skirt bit into her skin and seams popped as she crawled up his body and wrapped her legs around his lean waist. The ridge of his cock pushed the saturated silk of her panties against her clit, teasing her with the gentle rasp as he bucked against her.

He walked them to the corner of the room and fell to his knees, dropping her onto the seat of a wide armchair. Buttons flew and her blouse was turned to rags as Lucian ripped it free. Her bra and panties suffered a similar fate, but her skirt he left rucked up around her hips.

His hand was so tan against her pale breast. The contrast

of dark and light and the roughness of his palm on her soft skin made her sheath clench in anticipation of exploring their other differences.

Lucian palmed her generous mounds and pressed them together. He buried his face into her cleavage and drew a deep breath before taking both nipples into his mouth. The sounds of his sucking mouth and the little growls rumbling from his throat made her smile. Who knew the general was a breast man?

She cradled his head, gasping at the tug of his teeth on the turgid tips. Her hands moved to his shoulders where her fingertips found the raised flesh that spanned the broad width of his back. These scars he bore when he stood by his brother. These were scars of honor and courage. The matching slash across the tattoo on his biceps only began to speak of the suffering he endured at the hands of her father. Tears pricked her eyes that a thoughtless act of one man made Lucian doubt his purpose.

Cool air chilled her skin as he pulled away. Concern deepened the line between his eyebrows and dimmed the glow in his emerald eyes.

Amaryllis clutched at his arms. "Don't stop. I need you, Lucian. I need you inside me."

She spread her legs, hooking a knee over each of the chair's arms. The length of his cock rested on her belly, reaching almost to her navel. She reached down and maneuvered the flared crest to the entrance of her pussy and rolled her hips.

"Take me, Lucian. Watch as your cock splits me in two."

His gaze fell to the wet folds that bathed the head of his cock, and they both watched as he fed the crimson stalk into her sheath. The burn was incredible and made her pussy flood with more liquid heat to assist in the invasion. Deeper and deeper he pushed until he was buried to the hilt. His lips curled with a snarl as he withdrew all the way then slammed back inside her. The pounding rhythm made her back arch and her channel clench tight around the shuttling cock.

With a long, deep sigh, Amaryllis gave her entire body over to Lucian's desire. Her head rested against the back of the chair and her legs fell wider apart. Through half-lidded, sex-drugged eyes she admired the spectacular man before her. Sweat glistened and highlighted the dips and angles of his body. The muscles of his stomach flexed with each hard thrust of his hips. A tic in his jaw beat as he watched her revel in his possession. She drew her hands up her torso and cupped her breasts. Massaging the mounds, she flicked at the tight nipples with her fingernails.

The flaring of Lucian's nostrils was her only warning before he increased the force of his thrusts, making her cry out. The chair scraped along the floor with each of his lunges until stopped by the wall. He knocked her hands away from her breasts and claimed the mounds as his own. His rough palms kneaded the heavy weight as his nimble fingers twisted the tips, making her eyes roll back with the exquisite pleasure.

With each plunge, the chair butted against the wall, making the entire house shudder. The delicious curve of his cock struck along every nerve ending and pressed the head against a secret spot she didn't know she possessed. The rolling wave of lust she rode tossed her into rougher waters and sucked her into an abyss of sex and need that had her screaming. Her hands landed on his chest, her fingernails curling into his skin for purchase. Under her palms his two hearts beat frantically, and beneath her own chest it was like a bonfire had been lit and set her skin ablaze.

Broken grunts and stammered words like "tight" and "wet" and "fuck" fell from his lips in both English and Skandavian. Blood rushed through her ears, deafening her to his praises and hers. She could feel her lips moving, but whether to beg for more or cry out in surrender, she hadn't a clue.

Lucian's eyes widened in shock. His head tipped back and his mouth fell open to release a groan she felt ripped from her own gut. His fingers dug into her breast and his cock twitched in her pussy as he released his hot fluid with a series of furious thrusts. Seeing her straitlaced general at his feral-base nature made her channel clamp down as the first strikes of electricity radiated from her core.

"Lucian," she screamed through tight vocal cords and she swore a physical manifestation of her orgasm appeared as a white and blue light swirled around her and Lucian before exploding in a burst of sparks.

She closed her eyes tight against the brilliance and the deep-seated knowledge that being with Lucian had somehow changed her forever.

Chapter Six

S OMETHING WAS WRONG, very wrong, and her discomfort wasn't due to the tenderness between her thighs or the raw ache of her nipples.

She knew once the civilized veneer of Lucianllanos was removed, he'd become the rutting beast of her wildest fantasies. Since his return into her life, she thought of nothing but what it would be like to experience the taste of his kiss and the touch of his big hands. Now that she had, the new consuming question was when could she experience it again. He ruined her for any other man, human and non. Who would have thought it possible?

Yes, life as she knew it had changed, yet that wasn't what sent a shiver of foreboding down her spine.

She opened her eyes to see the bundle of wood and stuffing that remained of the chair he had claimed her on. Was it possible to have the piece repaired so that they could destroy it the same way again?

The bedside clock glowed six a.m. *Ack jus*, when was the last time she slept for so long? With the warm, comforting arms of Lucian holding her tight, a nice evening of cuddling after a round of incredible sex was something she could get used to.

Speaking of Lucian, where was her fierce warrior? The last image she remembered before falling into an orgasm-induced coma was the green blaze of his eyes as he lifted her onto his bed and pulled the sheet up to her chin. That same sheet was now cold with the absence of his heat.

The rise to consciousness was slow, but that nagging unease of a thousand pins pricking her belly prodded her the rest of the way to full wakefulness.

From the shadows, the sound of rhythmic slapping reached her ears. The longer she listened, the faster her breaths came until her lungs hurt. The sharp sound she recognized of leather hitting flesh. It was a noise she heard at least ten times a night in her club, but why was she hearing it now in Lucian's home?

She gathered the sheet around her naked body and slipped from the high bed. Using her ears like sonar, she crept one small step at a time in the direction of the noise.

A thin strip of light glowed under the closed bathroom door. As she approached, her pulse pounded hard and fast and her mouth went dry. Chills shook her even as sweat gathered above her lip.

A thick shell of determination dampened the agony of whoever was behind that door. Had Bale found them and was exacting his revenge on Lucian? Between Lucian's honor and the stories of Bale's ruthlessness, it wouldn't surprise her if Lucian offered himself in exchange for her life, while Bale left her broken with the knowledge she allowed Lucian to die while she slept in languid peace in the next room.

Well, she may have been born to a life where she wasn't expected to lift a finger, but she possessed the ability to kick ass when required. Despite the tremble in her hand, she reached for the doorknob and pushed.

Dear Gods.

Blood and mayhem she expected, but this…what twisted hell was this?

Lucian knelt on the floor, stripped of clothes and dignity. The blue tile floor was spotted with the blood that dripped from hundreds of lacerations on his back. In his hands he gripped the handle of a cat o' nine tails that scored the meat of his back with the flick of his wrist.

A sharp cry escaped from her tight throat, drawing his gaze to meet hers in the mirror. Self-recrimination shadowed his eyes that lacked the fire they had when he was buried inside her and immersed in the heat of their joining.

Never before had she been struck dumb. Not even when she was told she had to leave her homeland or when she heard of her mother's death had every molecule in her body turned to stone. Even her brain ceased to function.

Lucian turned on his knees and bent to kiss her feet. Blood and sweat marred the white sheet. "My princess. I beg your forgiveness. While I cannot change what has happened, know I am deeply sorry for my actions. I am not worthy to be in your presence. Please, I gladly take your punishment."

In his open palms, he offered the cat o' nine tails and bowed his head in supplication.

To see a man who commanded thousands, who leveled a platoon of revolutionaries with only a blaster and a sword, brought to his knees because he gave in to a need they both shared, pierced her hearts like a serrated blade. His shame was a blistering slap in the face that stunned as much as it ignited her fury.

How dare he. How dare he! A volcano of rage and hurt erupted from her chest and stung her eyes before she wrestled the pain back into its padlocked box and turned the key. He took her pleasure. He would not have her pain.

She reached for the whip, the handle stained dark with the blood that now coated her hand. Lucian may be contrite now, but she knew the truth he refused to acknowledge. He wanted her last night and reveled in every moment of their joining. This newfound remorse was an insult and he was a fool to think she'd tolerate one second of it.

"You are right. You are not worthy to touch me." Her grip tightened on the pommel. She raised her hand and threw the whip against the wall, smashing several tiles and punching a hole in the dry wall. "How could I have ever lowered myself to be with someone as cowardly as you? You are a disgrace to the *Llanos* name."

He lifted his head, grief tightened his features as he implored, "My princess."

"No. I am not your anything. Do not come near me again.

As of now, you no longer exist."

She ran from the room, racing straight down the stairs and out the door wearing nothing but the bed sheet. The lack of clothing didn't bother her, and to stop and grab clothes would only drag out her embarrassment. She had been stripped bare. No amount of clothing would change that.

✦   ✦   ✦

"HOLY SHIT," BRETT greeted when she opened the door. "Looks like you had quite the night."

Lucian knew what she saw on her doorstep. A sad man, unshaven, rumpled and in so much physical and mental pain he couldn't stand straight.

Amaryllis' barriers were good, but not even the strongest steel could stop him from feeling the burning pain he unintentionally caused.

It was his job to protect the princess so she could shine as the Gods intended. That was the job of *Llanos*. Not to sample her bounty. Not to lose his focus and leave them exposed. His honor fell to his libido, but his disgust lay solely with himself, never on Amaryllis.

The princess didn't hide or make apologies for who she was, which was a sexy, smart and vibrant woman who consumed life like a decadent buffet. Those very qualities made her the spectacular woman she was. He failed her as guard by crossing that line. An act punishable by death, and she had every right to demand his blood.

But Amaryllis never did anything as expected. With his misguided sense of righteousness, he hurt her more deeply than taking a molten blade to her flesh. An outcome he regretted more deeply than making love to her. While she refused to inflict punishment, he most solidly deserved it. His back looked like ground chuck but he would heal. The wound he inflicted upon her, he feared might never.

"Tell me she's here." Not only had he cut her to the quick, he also left her vulnerable to Bale. Another failure.

"Yes, she's here, or at least the blur of sheet that raced through here earlier makes me think it was her. And now that scene makes so much more sense." She stepped back and waved her hand. "Come on in. Kristos is making breakfast and Amaryllis is in the shower."

The thought of Amaryllis in the shower, washing off his touch, his possession, was another stab of agony. What he wanted and what was right tore him into so many pieces, who knew if he could be put back together into a semblance of the man he once was. Instinct made him want to interrupt her shower and re-mark her with his essence. Temperance demand he allow her time to dress and see him when she wasn't at her most vulnerable. The little honor he clung to won out and let her be.

"Would you like some coffee?" Brett asked as she led him into the kitchen.

"No, thank you."

"Hey, brother." Kristos looked up from the skillet of eggs

he was supervising. "Mother of all! You've—"

"Kristos," Brett slapped his arm. "Lucian's had a hard night. Let's not make his morning difficult."

Lucian winced at the phrase "hard night". He fell onto a seat at the table and dropped his head in his hands.

"I can't believe you had sex with the princess." Kristos sat on the chair across from him.

"Is it that obvious?"

He shot his wife an incredulous look over his shoulder. She scowled and shook her head, which led to an unspoken argument between the pair consisting of head shakes, pinched foreheads and shrugged shoulders.

Kristos slashed at the air with a definitive hand and turned to him to ask, "Was it that bad?"

Lucian snorted mirthlessly. "Quite the opposite."

"Let me take a wild guess." Brett placed a glass of orange juice and a plate of toast on the table before him and took her own seat. "After a mutually enjoyable evening, you said something only a *Llanos* would say."

He closed his eyes and nodded. "I didn't mean to hurt her. She is my princess and I her guard. She knows we can never be."

"Why not?" She placed her hand over his. "Lucian, have you realized that the only person who insists on drawing that line is you? If you like her, do something about it."

"Are you the same woman who had to face death in order to realize her feelings for my brother?"

The tilt of her head dared him to speak further. "Learn from my experience."

"Kristos, you understand. Talk to your woman."

Kristos swallowed a short laugh and reached for Brett's hand. "*Alskata*, there are rules in the Skandavian court that you do not break. As you know, punishment sometimes meant death. Our ways are very traditional and may appear antiquated, but the princess's consort may one day rule the kingdom, and as such, her contact with men is highly scrutinized. However, as it's been pointed out many times, this is not Skandavia. So what's really holding you back, Luc?"

"Are you serious? Have you forgotten there is an assassin after us? After her? How can I protect her if all I am thinking about is…" A vision of her full breasts bouncing with his every thrust into her rippling sheath flashed before him. He blinked hard to clear the image from his overworked mind and saw his family staring at him with a mixture of surprise and amusement on their faces. "I will not let my affection for her place her in danger."

"And you won't," Brett argued. "Because you love her. Don't deny it. We can all see that you do, Lucian. That's why you're so upset. Love her, protect her, but Jesus, don't smother her."

"Plus, you have us," Kristos added. "I remember a somewhat smart man once asked me if it was more important to be right or to have Brett."

"Do not throw my words back at me."

"What are you so afraid of?"

Afraid? Him? Inconceivable.

Or was it?

Amaryllis reminded him that to live was more than his hearts beating and meaningless conversations. Life was a series of experiences that made your blood fire and stirred your passion. She reminded him what it was to *feel*. To love. To obtain that joy, to share in a love so powerful was a precious gift. And to have that love taken away would leave him shattered. He had his entire existence stripped away before and no amount of dermabrasion could smooth away the scar of that loss. Perhaps he was afraid to feel, truly feel, for fear of losing it all again.

Tragic events happened to people all the time. The brave ones rose above the chaos and not only kept going but found the strength to laugh, to love, to do more than merely exist from day to day. He had once thought of himself as courageous. Could he draw on that courage now to claim what he wanted for his very own?

As if Amaryllis would even give him the chance, he thought bitterly.

"What I want no longer matters. She won't acknowledge I exist."

"That's because you hurt her feelings. She cares for you, Lucian," Brett said. "I know I've only just met her, but Amaryllis strikes me as a woman who not only hurts deeply but loves deeply too. Talk to her. Tell her what's in your heart and ask for her forgiveness."

"It's not that simple." He shook his head. Brett hadn't felt the burning stab of betrayal he had when he offered his whip.

A knowing smirk created a dimple in her cheek as she pulled the cellphone from her pocket. "Hold still." She snapped a picture of him and turned the screen in his direction.

All he could do was stare in profound shock at the photo that captured his eyes. Not possible. Not now. Irises that were usually a deep green of cut emeralds were now milky white.

"Congratulations, brother!" Kristos slapped him on the back, yet Lucian didn't even flinch at the sting, he was so stupefied. "You've bonded. Or at least have begun the process. Now you just have to get the girl. Piece of cake."

Lucian arched an incredulous brow. How was this possible? "I didn't speak the words."

"Well, one of you did and the other was somewhat agreeable or else your eyes wouldn't have changed."

True. Lucian looked in the direction of the guest bath where his woman's anger pulsed, despite the barriers she used to temper it.

Convince her that she had joined herself to him in an emotional bond so strong, it carried on beyond death?

Right. Piece of cake.

✦　　✦　　✦

JESU, DID HER eyes burn. Amaryllis pressed the cotton bath

towel to the throbbing orbs and pushed until they felt ready to burst from their sockets.

She never cried over a man before and she'd be damned if she shed one more tear for that unfeeling asshole. Well, that wasn't entirely true. He had felt something. Guilt and regret.

"Bastard," she muttered and mustered all of her strength into shutting her hurt and all thoughts about Lucian into a lead box, never to be opened again.

Men had always held a specific purpose in her life. Pleasure and protection. Lucian was the only man to effectively blur the line and cross into the unchartered territory of companion. For the first time she wanted to give her heart to a man and share more than her body with another. She wanted to find out his dreams and do all in her power to make them come true. Make him smile with joy and not just leer with lust. Although the lust was a delicious bonus.

No, no, no! She squeezed her thighs against the electric sizzle of need that took residence in her empty sheath. Best sex of her life? Yes. But if she had to sleep with every man on this planet, and the next, to replace the experience, she would.

Good plan, but you know that won't work. He's ruined you.

Never. Not acceptable. There had to be a way to erase the memory of that damn *Llanos.*

Speaking of which. The sour taste of his guilt slipped down her throat. He was here, in the house.

Why? Did he think she hadn't received the message that she wasn't wanted loud and clear? Fuck him if he thought she would listen to another feeble excuse that he wasn't worthy of her touch.

Well, he could sit there until she was good and ready to face him, which may not be ever, and definitely not until she was primped and polished to an immaculate shine.

She tossed the towels into the hamper then attacked her hair with a brush and dryer. A wild tangle of silken locks blew in all directions, highlighting the sight that made her hand freeze mid-stroke. Blood rushed in her ears and her lungs struggled to function as she leaned close to the mirror and fingered the two-inch-wide lock of black hair that grew from her nape under her left ear. From root to tip, the once-blonde strands were a pitch black that shimmered with a blue halo. Lucian black.

Bastard. Self-righteous prick, son-of-*puntahi shittehoar*. That *pundavii* had the nerve to speak the Sacred Vows then deny her with the next breath? The gall! The *cajones*!

How utterly, utterly hurtful.

Disappointment broke through her shock and brought forth a fresh set of tears. She had thought when a man spoke the Sacred Vows, she would at least remember it.

In her youth the moment had been dreamt about with candlelight and romantic music. Her fantasy had her re-splendent in silk and primped to perfection as the man she loved settled between thighs she held spread wide in welcome. As he thrust into her body, he'd cup her breasts while looking deep into her eyes and speak the words that would bind their emotions together forever.

Never had she imagined that such a momentous event would take place with her sprawled in an armchair, half clothed and panting like a bitch in heat, or that she wouldn't hear the words at all. Then as an added insult have her mate reject her the next morning. That's probably why the bond was only partially complete.

Fool! Of course a life-altering occasion in her life would be thus. That was her curse.

If he had come to beg her forgiveness in this, he was fucking insane. And in front of his family? The humiliation would be too much to bear. The seven levels of hell would turn into a five-star beach resort before she faced him again.

She brushed the worst of the tangles free and tied her hair into a low ponytail, disguising as much of the black strands as possible.

Rushing to her suitcase, she threw on the first items she touched then snatched up her purse and went to the window. She could send for the rest of her things later.

The possibility that she could be heading right into Bale's wicked clutches didn't stop her flight. Let him take her. Then perhaps the excruciating pain in her chest would finally ease.

Not a twig snapped nor pine needle stirred as she raced through the forest. She ran so fast, she didn't even disturb the dew on the grass.

A quick glance at the store front of the Cedar Sports and Marine confirmed Harlan was busy with the morning rush of fishermen. She traced to the main house and pounded on the front door.

Dhavin answered. His smile faded as he took stock of her from head to toe. "What happened?"

She breezed past him. "Good morning to you too."

"Amaryllis. What happened?"

"I need to go home. My home. Now."

"Where's Lucian or Kristos?"

She stopped his entreaty with a firm shake of her head. "Please, Dhavin. If you've loved me at all, even if all you felt was the compassion reserved for a mere acquaintance, I beg of you, take me home. No questions."

Dhavin took one of her hands in both of his and stared into her eyes. All she wanted was to look away in disgrace but she mustered the courage to hold his gaze and silently implored him to comply with her wishes. She knew she was asking him to not only defy his commander but his family as well. A request she had no right making, and she would not blame him if he refused, but he was all she had to rely on.

After several long seconds he offered her half a smile and nodded. "I won't take you home, but I'll take you someplace else. You will tell me everything once we are there. Promise me."

"Of course." A small request in return for his loyalty.

"Give me three minutes to pack some essentials. Do you have an alternative location in mind?"

"Yes." She stopped him with a hand on his arm. "Thank

you, Dhavin."

He kissed her cheek then fell to one knee with head bowed. "You are my friend as well as my princess. You will always be able to call upon me."

Unable to speak lest she fall completely apart, she bent and kissed his forehead, lamenting that her bonded mate was not the brave man kneeling before her now but the coward who had knelt at her feet and stabbed her in the hearts. The very hearts she feared belonged to him forever.

Chapter Seven

B ALE HALTED INSIDE the threshold of The Cavern. A blast of emotions slammed into his chest with the force of a battering ram, knocking him back a step. Humans, even the most reserved of the species, projected their every feeling as if they were standing with a microphone on a parade float loaded with speakers turned to eleven. The cacophony of mental noise rocketing through his brain was an unexpected obstacle he hadn't prepared to face. It was a transparent weapon with the potential of bringing him to his knees if he wasn't careful.

"Having second thoughts, my man?" the man monitoring the door asked. "I don't care where you go, but you gotta clear the way."

He nodded and slid into a corner to strengthen his mental barricade. The pulsating beat coming from the sound system was just as overwhelming as the barrage of emotions. Drawing in a deep breath, then another, he concentrated on slowing down his heartbeats and focusing on where the flat, dead places in the atmosphere lay. Even though the princess had been well known for her inability to lock down her emotions, she would have had to gain some control in order to survive in such chaos. Those breaks would be where she resided.

Under his leather jacket and hooded sweatshirt, sweat trickled down his back, and the scent of sex and alcohol added to the claustrophobia. Bodies gyrated everywhere he looked. On the dance floor, at the bar, in the dark corners and on tabletops. This place was a den of vice and, frankly, he was quite surprised that a royal, even Princess Amaryllis, would consort with such heathens.

He wove through the crowd, trying his best not to come into contact with anyone. The restaurant his interrogations had led him to earlier was more in style of an exiled royal, while this place reminded him of the underground lairs his fellow guardsmen frequented when horny and without a wife to sate their baser needs, not that he visited such locations himself. At least not after he had wed Natalia. Sexually she was more delicate in her desires than he had been used to and the Gods knew she deserved better than the likes of him. But Natalia was perfect in her fragility and provided all he had needed. Even the simple act of stepping across the threshold to such a salacious establishment sent a rotten-egg taste shooting down his throat with the thought he was offending her spirit.

A wee girl jumped before him, startling him with her boldness. She was rail-thin with hair so black it absorbed all light. The makeup around her eyes was just as dark and her lips were stained with a layer of red. Leather straps criss-crossed her body, barely covering her intimate areas.

"Are you in need of a slave?" she asked, running her palms

over her breasts and down her sides.

"No." He moved to step around her.

She stepped with him, matching him zig for zag. "I offer myself willingly. I promise I'll do whatever you ask."

Obviously. "No."

"Please, Master."

"Stop." He held his hand an inch from her nose. "You want to please me?"

"Yes," she panted.

"Tell me where to find the—Amaryllis."

"The chick who owns the joint?"

Owner? How absolutely depraved. "Is there more than one by that name?"

"Well, no."

"Where is she?"

"Don't know. Haven't seen her. But when she's not on the dance floor she's usually up in her private room." She pointed up to an empty balcony.

A grand staircase swept up to a catwalk that led to the princess' sanctum. One guard, if you could call him that, stood at the bottom, Bale's only obstacle to the top.

"Stay," he said to the pixie. When she opened her mouth, he silenced her with a sharp, "Stay."

She nodded, her eyes wide and dreamy. Without a second thought he left the pest and used his newfound powers to race from shadow to shadow. He easily slipped past the guard and stalked down the hallway, pausing at each door to look for his prey.

More debauchery infiltrated the corners of the club. Women were bound in all manners of restraint while men fondled and subjugated them to their whims.

Bale peered into the third room and came to a halt, instantly captivated by the scene taking place. One step, then another. His feet moved of their own accord, drawing him closer to the display.

On a small platform stood a man stripped bare and illuminated by several floor lamps. His hands were strapped to a bar high above his head, stretching out his torso like a canvas ready to be painted upon. The stark light washed out his skin tone to a bluish-white, yet his cock throbbed a deep red where it jutted out at full-staff from his groin.

A woman circled her captive. A vision of hedonistic delight herself, she was a walking wet dream. Long, thick chestnut hair waved down her back. Her makeup was applied with a more sophisticated hand than the pixie he ran into earlier, and her leather corset cupped her curves like a jealous lover. The short-shorts encasing her hips exposed the bottom of her fleshy ass cheeks, which jiggled with her every step as she padded barefoot across the stage. She made her slave widen his stance so she could better test the weight of his hard cock and heavy sac.

"Who do you belong to?" she asked in a low voice as smoky as the finest tobacco.

"You, Sir."

That the male addressed her with such a title shocked Bale more than anything he had seen on this planet thus far. Surely a woman would be insulted to be addressed as a man, but the satisfaction in this female's smile belied his assumption.

The heavy allure of anticipation tightened his throat and raised his body temperature another twenty degrees until he was forced to loosen the zipper of his sweatshirt, desperate he was for some modicum of breath. Bale's mental barriers trembled. His powers absorbed the slave's excitement until the man's desire became his own.

"Will you take your punishment?" the woman asked with a scrape of her nails down the inside of his thigh.

He swallowed hard. "Yes Sir."

Bale watched, entranced that such a small woman could command a male so much larger than she. When she picked up a whip, he gasped. His lungs billowed hard until his harsh breath matched in rhythm while the slave's eyes glittered with desperate hunger.

Crack! The whip flew, striking bare flesh. Bale felt the hot lick of leather across his own back and clenched his teeth against a moan. He curled his hands into fists so tight his nails dug into his palms.

Another lash fell, then another. With each strike the slave's pleasure grew, reaching across the room to squeeze Bale around the chest. The pure joy of giving yourself over to another washed over him, hardening his cock to the point that the bite of his zipper digging into his erection brought its own twisted sense of pleasure, and with it the envy that he was not the one on the receiving end of the whip.

"Good boy," the Master cooed. "You've earned your reward."

A woman from the crowd stepped up onto the stage. She knelt at the slave's feet and released her breasts from her corset. At the Master's command, the newcomer wrapped her hands around the slave's cock and stroked him from base to tip with firm strokes.

"Come on her tits," the Master commanded.

The slave tossed his head back and screamed as white jets of cum squirted on the full globes of his target.

Bale grabbed his own cock and squeezed so hard his eyes watered and his vision went dim. He stumbled from the room, blind to all but the shock wave of euphoria that rippled from the trio. Falling against the wall, he bent in two and fought to regain his composure.

This wasn't happening. He didn't feel emotions of his own. The experience was too raw, left him too vulnerable. This demand to be dominated burning through his veins was absolutely deplorable and had to end. Now.

"Hey, man. Are you okay?" a male voice asked.

Bale waited for the footsteps to grow closer before he whirled around and pinned the man to the wall with his forearm across the fragile windpipe. He pulled out a thin blade from his back pocket and dug the tip into the man's side.

"Where is Amaryllis?" he growled, ready for this shit mission to be over.

The man's eyebrows rose. "Don't know."

"Where. Is. She?"

"I don't know." The man gasped and dug his fingers into Bale's arm as he pressed deeper into his neck.

His powers sensed the truth, but that didn't mean this human didn't know vital information. He twisted the blade, neatly slicing into soft tissue. A sharp stab of agony traveled from the human to Bale, who soaked up the pain-laced adrenaline like a much-needed jolt of reality. "What *do* you know?"

Sweat beaded on his brow and dripped into frightened blue eyes. "She told me an enemy of her father's may be after her and she was going to lie low. She refused to tell me where she was going so that I couldn't be used against her."

He grunted in reply. So the princess knew she was being hunted. How? "Smart girl. Did she leave on her own?"

A pause. "Yes."

Lie. "Who did she go with?"

"I don't know."

Bale lifted the blade. With his eyes locked on the human's, he licked at the blood coating the metal. The man chocked on a gurgling whimper and trembled violently. "Do I need to repeat the question?"

"There was a man here the other night. Big. Dark. Like you. She might have gone with him."

Lucian? Could it be? Had his former mentor continued

with his duty of protecting royalty, even after being publicly denounced by their king? The man had always been a self-righteous prat who never budged from the rules. How thoughtful of his old friend to make Bale's mission easier by staying with his target.

Bale released his hold, but only by a little. He narrowed his gaze and whispered, "If I were you, I would do all I could to contact Amaryllis. Tell her that an admirer is looking for her, and if she wants to see her dear friend again, she will meet me here, and bring her protector with her. If she refuses, then I will slaughter every person under this roof. Starting with you."

He backed away, turning as his informant slid down the wall. The trap was baited, all there was to do was wait.

Escape from this rotting hell-hole was his next priority. These humans were like parasites, digging into the psyche to leach his blood and lay eggs of depravity to fester in his mind.

Shouts of indignation rippled behind him as he stumbled through the club, knocking into revelers and other heathens in his search for the nearest exit. The blessed rain slapped him in the face as he burst out onto the street, but the sting wasn't nearly enough. So he ran, and ran, deeper into the city where few dared to tread on their own, to where the stench of sex turned into the stench of human decay and hopelessness.

His skin cooled, but his blood still thundered in his ears. Above the mad rush in his head came the sound of a pleading cry and the sensation of fire ants crawling over his skin. A presence of malice.

Around the corner Bale spotted a cluster of men. They surrounded two others, one who lay on the ground and another who stood defiantly. Such courage called to him like a beacon in the dark.

As Bale approached, he heard their conversation, and the lust for flesh turned into the lust for blood. Now this he was familiar with.

"Stay away from my brother," the defiant one shouted, revealing her to be female, to Bale's surprise. "He told you we don't have any money."

"Too bad, bitch," the ringleader replied. "His big mouth got Tony busted, and now I'm out of a sale. He owes me. Kick him again," he ordered one of his men.

"No!" The girl jumped on top of her brother, shielding him with her tiny body.

"If you don't have my money, then I'm taking it out of his ass, and yours too, baby." The leader laughed, rubbing at his crotch with one hand while grabbing the girl by the hair with the other.

"Enough," Bale commanded. "Let her go."

The entire group froze as his voice echoed down the alley. The leader gave him a visual once-over. A sliver of terror widened his eyes as he took in Bale's size, but he quickly recovered and sneered, "Stay out of this, old man. This ain't none of your business."

"I'm making it my business. Let her go."

"Yeah?" the leader asked, all balls and bravado. He pulled

an object from his waistband and aimed it as Bale's chest. From the shape it reminded Bale of his blaster, probably functioned the same way too. "Well I say it ain't."

That's right. Give me a reason. Bale drew a deep breath, filling his lungs with the anticipation of battle. He withdrew his short-sword from the scabbard strapped to his back, which for some reason sent a ripple of amused laughter through the group of thugs.

"Nice sword, geek boy. Gonna try to go medieval on me, uh? Are you faster than a speeding bullet?"

"Yes."

Swoosh. The soft slice of a quick blade was drowned out by hysterical screaming as the leader dropped to his knees, clutching the stump where his hand was once attached to his arm.

The girl shrieked, scrambling back like a crab while dragging the semiconscious body of her brother with her across the asphalt. "Don't kill me. Please, don't kill me."

"Run," Bale growled. "You've been traumatized enough without having to witness what I'm about to do. Run!"

Once the girl and her brother safely away, Bale turned to bask in the chaos he set in motion. Without their commander, the felons didn't know which way to piss. A few withdrew their own guns and held them in trembling grips while some were frozen in horrified shock. Another was a quarter-mile down the road in the fastest sprint he probably ever ran in his young life. But Bale was faster.

Three more feet was all the man traveled before Bale had him by the arm and dragged him back to his mates.

Tossing the crying man to the ground, Bale spat at his feet. "I do not like you. You are like the foulest of gutter beasts and have no worth on this or any other planet. It is my honor to rid the universe of the likes of you."

Bullets flew yet none found their target as Bale swirled and dodged with his sword flying in graceful arcs. Blood splattered across his face and coated his hands while the terrified shouts of the damned rang in his ears like a beautiful symphony.

Now this was his element. Death was the lover he was most attuned with. Nothing else mattered. Nothing.

"Halt! In the name of Queen Moira Eleanna Rosenorn, I command you to stop and put down the weapons."

Bale wiped at the blood dripping in his eyes and peered into the shadows. "Show yourself, you coward."

A black-hooded figure shimmered under the lone lamp illuminating the street. To the untrained eye, a *Llanos* guard appeared interchangeable from the next. The uniform was designed to prevent the enemy from knowing who exactly they were engaging. But like a mother able to tell her newborn twins apart, Bale knew who approached by the tilt of his head, the high grip on the pommel of his sword and how he led with his right foot.

"Kristos, the failure. How kind of you to respond to my message so quickly, although I was hoping your brother would attend as well."

"Let's go meet him now. Drop the sword and come quietly."

"I will never go quietly. Come and get me."

One second Kristos was across the street and in the next he was in front of Bale, connecting a right hook to his jaw that sent him flying into a nearby street lamp.

Super powers gained by entering Earth's atmosphere. Confirmed. Higher ability to withstand pain. Negative.

Bale rolled to the right, narrowly missing the edge of Kristos' blade. Sparks struck where the metal met the pavement. With the gun out of reach, he sprang to his feet and withdrew a dagger from his waist. The *Llanos* had the advantage of the local's weaponry yet he did not use it. Idiot.

Blade clanged against blade in a musical cacophony that resembled wind chimes caught in a storm. Kristos attacked with the grace of his training, but the years of inaction showed as Bale caught him with a strike against his ribs he was slow to recover from.

"Lie down and die with what little dignity you have left, Kristos."

"I'm not nearly done," he shouted and turned to run, racing right up the side of a building to tuck into a back flip and land behind Bale.

"Dude, did you see that?"

More shouts and exclamations followed, bringing Bale's attention to outside the battle arena. Drawn by the sound of combat, the humans had come out of their apartments and nearby taverns to stand on the sidewalks and shimmy up drain pipes to watch the embattled warriors. Unsure of what they were witnessing or who to root for, the crowd watched with an abundance of emotions that ranged from terror at the use of their deadly skill to being awestruck at their speed and talent. With his emotional barrier already weak, each additional response created a tumultuous cloud that covered Bale and rained down in broken glasslike shards that ripped his control to shreds.

Kristos landed a kick to the head, followed by a punch to the kidneys that had Bale coughing up blood. Between the physical and mental bombardment, he was losing focus. He was failing.

The wail of sirens brought both men up short and made Bale shield his eyes as vehicles came screaming around the corner to surround him with bright lights flashing. Doors popped open as more humans dressed in military-style uniforms drew their blasters and pointed them at the two men.

"Drop your weapons," one of the newcomers shouted.

Ah, so that is where Kristos learned that ridiculous command.

"Death first," he bellowed and turned. If Kristos could climb walls, so could he.

He ran full steam toward the side of a brick building and scaled the side in seconds. Once on the roof he turned to look down at the gathering masses and pointed to Kristos who remained illuminated in the vehicle's headlights.

"We are not finished, Kristos. My family demands the blood of you and your kin. Take heed, citizens. This man's blood is mine and any who attempt to stop me will die with him. I will have my revenge!"

To retreat made his stomach churn and the bile rise in his throat, but better to regroup and fight another day. By right or by might, he would not fail. His family would be avenged. If that meant destroying the entire planet to achieve that, so be it.

Chapter Eight

"HOW IS SHE?" Lucian asked his cousin the moment he appeared in his car's headlights.

Dhavin widened his stance and folded his arms over his chest. "Amaryllis is being Amaryllis. She's wearing a brave face, but I know inside she's weeping. She's too proud to let rejection from her mate keep her down."

"I didn't reject her. Is that what she thinks?" Lucian barked then snapped his mouth shut. He wiped his hand over his face. The only person he had to convince of his sincerity was Amaryllis, any other arguing was wasted energy. "Where is she? Or is the only reason you brought me one hundred fifty miles from Cedar to berate me?"

He narrowed his eyes and swept a considering gaze over Lucian. "I wanted to see your face, feel you, if you tried to deny your bond."

"I'm not denying it. Just trying to understand it myself."

"And what do you propose to do about it?"

Lucian met his cousin's stare. "I'm claiming my woman, if she'll have me."

Dhavin nodded. "A half mile down the road. Cottage 57. Belongs to a girlfriend of hers who's out of the country, so you won't be disturbed. I'll keep an eye out for our friend."

"Thank you, cousin."

"Make her happy."

Lucian held out his hand, palm up, fingers curled. Dhavin wrapped his fingers around Lucian's, creating the circle shape. They slid their palms down and grasped each other around the forearm and bent at the waist in a warrior's bow.

The gesture was a sign of respect, a far different emotion than the sheer terror and unadulterated fury Lucian had felt when he discovered his mate and his cousin had disappeared from right under his nose. Anger and wounded pride had quickly given way to panic and fear, which had increased the longer he spent searching the countryside for the pair. The only thing that barely tempered his anxiety was the knowledge that Dhavin would lay down his life for the princess. And hell yes, was Lucian ever jealous of the connection they shared.

An Amaryllis-sized hole had exploded in his chest when he realized she'd rather face a deadly assassin than her bonded mate. The hole festered with a silent burn, reminding him of what he stood to lose.

Once he regained her forgiveness and earned her love, then he would take great pleasure in reminding her that as her mate, it was his honor to be everything for her.

Lucian got into his car and took off down the street, counting the house numbers as he passed. As he approached 57 he felt the urge to smile for the first time in days. Leave it to Amaryllis to find a round house in a community of square cottages to reside in. He parked the car in the driveway and strode up the front porch, using the key Dhavin slipped him to unlock the door that was far too flimsy for his preference.

"What did you bring back? I'm starving." Amaryllis strolled in from the bath and stopped short when she saw him. Her eyes narrowed and her hands fell to her hips. "Go away."

Lucian stifled a sigh. Ya, she wasn't going to make this easy. "I'm sorry I hurt you this morning. I would have never done anything to disrespect the Sacred Vows you spoke."

She gasped with outrage before schooling her expression into a cool mask. "I don't know what you're talking about. And even if I did, I would never speak the Sacred Vows and most certainly not to you!"

He gestured to his face. "I may look it, but I'm not blind. We're bonded."

"Keep dreaming, soldier. I show no signs of any bond. Leave now."

He frowned as he inspected the damp strands of her hair held off the back of her neck in a loose knot. Not a single black strand was visible in the upswept hairstyle.

That made no sense. They were bonded just as sure as he was standing before her. The humiliation she suffered earlier was like a sticky web that clung as if freshly spun, entwining around him as if it were his own. Only as her bonded mate would he be able to feel the indecision tearing her in two so succinctly. Part of her wanted to run into his arms while the other wanted to drive her nails into his eyes.

Hopefully he'd be able to convince her his arms were a better choice. "That royal wave isn't going to make me leave."

She backed to the other side of the room as he stalked her. "I command you to leave now."

"Not until you hear me," he yelled when she dodged left around his outstretched hand. Catching the back of her shirt, he tackled her around the waist and fell to his knees so he didn't threaten her with his size.

"Let go of me."

"I love you."

That stopped her as effectively as a two-by-four to the head. Her eyes grew as large as dinner plates as she trembled in his arms. "You lie."

"No, Amaryllis. Feel me. Feel the truth in my words."

"Why? What do you hope to gain by speaking such lies?" The tears gathering in her eyes crushed him.

"Please. Two minutes. That's all I ask is two minutes."

He pressed his forehead against her sternum and took a moment to choose his words with care. So far he'd done nothing but put his foot in his mouth every time they had a conversation. Pretty speeches were not his forte, and now was not the time to be fancy. All he could give her was what was in his heart and pray it was enough.

"Amaryllis, you are a gift and everything a man could ever want. You are light. You are life. You are love. I lost it all once and the thought of losing you, it rips, it—" He stopped to swallow hard. "You were right to call me a coward. I was afraid to go after what I wanted, so I pushed you away. But life without you isn't a life at all. Please, give me another chance, Amaryllis." He stood and cupped her cheeks in his palms, his thumbs brushed at the tears clinging to her lashes. "I'm ready to be the man you need."

"You don't know what I need."

A chuckle welled in his throat. "I know exactly what you need."

Dhavin had told him. She herself told him many times. He had heard but he hadn't listened until he recognized that same need within himself. Amaryllis longed to belong. If she gave him her trust, she would never again doubt whom she belonged to.

The tremble shaking her shoulders turned into a full-out shudder as he leaned forward and brushed his lips over hers. Her eyes remained open, fixed on him in a combination of wonder and confusion. Never before had he experienced such softness, such an intoxicating blend of vulnerability and confidence that made him hunger to experience more.

The bitter taste of her fear rode the edge of hope as he continued to drop butterfly kisses on her lips. He swept his tongue along the seam and pressed his advantage when she gasped with surprise. The night before he had been driven by the need to gorge himself on her taste. Tonight he intended to savor the sweetness of his princess.

He scooped her up in his arms and took the stairs to the loft bedroom two at a time. Amaryllis had a personality so large, he forgot just how small she was until he held her cradled to his chest.

"My *akita*," he breathed. His little one. "You are so precious to me."

"Lucian, this is insane. You hate me." She hiccupped softly.

"No. No, love, I've never hated you. Do you drive me crazy? Absolutely, but never have I hated you. Let me show you how much you mean to me." He set her on her feet then let out a low whistle as he took stock of his surroundings.

The bedroom was created for pleasures of the flesh, complete with a padded table, an array of whips and a complicated-looking swing. Thank the Gods Amaryllis' friend was female. As it was his mind was racing with fantasies he didn't want to think about her engaging in with anyone but him.

One thing was clear, his Amaryllis was an adventurous girl. If he pushed, she'd shove back with a rebel yell. Tonight he was going to give her exactly what she needed.

Using his super speed, he stripped the shirt and bra from her body, but slowed to release the clip from her hair and smooth the soft strands over her breasts.

Above their heads hung a metal bar trimmed with fur-lined cuffs. He kissed her palm then lifted her arm to strap her wrist in place and encouraged her fingers to wrap around the bar. Once her other wrist was secured, he quickly searched the nearby dresser and closet and gathered items that inspired his imagination.

Amaryllis watched him with wide eyes and a simmering arousal that reached out and stroked down his spine like a satin glove. He took his sweet time to undress, relishing the touch of her gaze as he slowly exposed his body. He ached to grip his throbbing cock to ease a bit of the pressure tightening his balls, but this time was for his mate.

"Lucian," she gasped. "Your back."

He looked over his shoulder to see his reflection in the mirrored closet door. Although he had healed considerably, the skin still held the welts from the whip and burned an angry red.

"I deserved it for hurting you. That and much more." He pressed a kiss to the frown marring her brow. "Don't think on it. I want your entire focus to be on the pleasure you bring me."

The pulse fluttering frantically on either side of her neck fascinated him and tickled his lips as he kissed a wet path down to her shoulder. The brush of her breasts against his chest as her breathing increased was a divine barometer of her rising desire. He slid her jeans and panties down her smooth legs then reached for two blocks he found in the closet and prompted her to stand upon them. On his way back up to a stand, he ran his palms over as much of her supple skin as he could reach. As he took the weight of her breasts in his hands, he restrained the urge to weep with joy and thanked the Gods for creating such perfection.

Amaryllis' curves had been a topic of discussion many

times amongst the men of the guard. Never in his wildest imagination did he ever believe he would be the one to have the right to explore the difference in texture between the satin of her nipple and the silk of her breast. "When I took the guard out on overnight missions, I would hear them whisper about you. Spinning tales of what they'd do to you if you were their woman. Their stories do not compare."

"And what of you, Lucian?" She sucked in a breath when he twisted both nipples. "Did you join in or did the general put his foot down on such blasphemous talk?"

"Of course my men were reprimanded, however…" A smile flirted on his lips before he sucked the puckered nub into his mouth.

To his men he might have appeared disgusted with their vulgarity, yet in his mind he was just as bad, if not worse than they had been. On more than one occasion he had taken himself in hand, imagining he was sliding into her well-oiled cleavage until he came in her waiting mouth. Usually a grueling twenty-mile run followed as punishment for his improper thoughts.

Not anymore. He trailed biting kisses down her belly as he knelt between her spread legs. Now he was free to feast on his bonded mate while reveling in the pulsing heat of her desire.

"Beautiful." He blew a stream of air onto her bare folds. The sight of her hunger was even more arousing than the hum buzzing from her powers.

She was soaking wet against his fingers as he parted her

labia and settled his mouth against the drenched portal. He nibbled at the nub of her clit and speared two fingers deep into her sheath, which eagerly suckled at his invasion. She was sweet and spicy, a flavor that inflamed him as much as it offered comfort that her taste now belonged solely to him.

Her thighs trembled and stuttered moans turned into frantic pants the harder he sucked on her clit. He curled his fingers and rubbed the soft spot in front of the neck of her womb.

"Lucian," she screamed.

A current of electricity shot from her pussy down his spine and along the length of his cock while her body jerked against his tongue. The ceiling creaked as she loosened the bolts of the bar with her orgasm, raining plaster down on their heads.

Lucian gripped the base of his cock and twisted, attempting to stave off the orgasm boiling in his balls. Pre-cum mixed with her cream on his fingers, increasing the need to release where he sat. Only his warrior training and determination to be balls-deep in his mate when he came kept him in check.

He used the edge of his tongue to gently bring her down from the heavens while keeping her primed for more pleasure.

When she caught her breath, he stood and pressed his lips to the spot under her ear. "Can you come for me again, *akita*?"

She licked her lips, swollen from where she bit them in an attempt to hold back her screams. Leaning forward, she licked her cream from his chin and shuddered. "Lucian. I hurt. Please. I need."

"Do you want to come again?" he whispered in her ear.

"Yes."

"Do you need to be fucked?"

"Yes," she cried.

"By who?"

She looked up at him with those luminous lavender eyes, drowsy and feverish. "You, Lucian. Only you."

"That's right."

He left her to retrieve the vibrator he left on top of the dresser. The purple toy was long and curved like a wavy cane. She flinched as he trailed the cold plastic down her torso and slipped the tip between the swollen folds of her pussy and into her cunt. In and out he stoked the phallus into her channel then nestled the crook against her clit and flipped on the switch.

Bumps erupted over her fair skin and the points of her nipples tightened along with his balls. He went back to the dresser and picked up a bottle of lubrication, squirting a generous amount on his hand to slather over his dripping cock. He kept his movements short, resisting the need to fuck his own hand.

She was so beautiful, stretched out, her breasts jiggling as she shook with need. The purple vibrator highlighting her glistening pussy lips was both tawdry and sensual at the same time. He stepped up behind her to watch her reflection as he pressed the tips of his fingers to the puckered hole of her ass and pushed deep. She took the invasion with ease, her head tipping back as she moaned and pressed into his hand.

"Have you been taken here?" he asked, thrusting and scissoring inside her.

"Yes, but not by anything as big as you."

"Are you scared?"

"No. Make it burn, Lucian."

Her words snapped the last of his control. Any intention of taking her easy was incinerated as she begged him to fuck her. Tucking the crown of his cock against the hole, he fed it inside her with short jabs of his hips.

Sweat poured down his face and his jaw ached from clenching his teeth together in concentration. The grip was so intense, his eyes crossed from the pleasure. Against the underside of his cock, the vibrator buzzed, sending flames up his spine. He was not going to last long. Already his cock twitched, ready to spill. With so little time left, he had to make this count.

Amaryllis writhed in his arms, going up on tiptoe with each slam of his hips. She gave as good as she got, pushing back and squeezing his cock with her muscles. His hands slipped over her skin, slick with perspiration. Cupping her breasts, he pinched the nipples and commanded, "Amaryllis. Look at us. Look at me."

When her gaze met his in the mirror, he curled around her back and buried himself to the base. He pulled back and drove deep and spoke the words that would complete the bond, if she accepted.

By the Gods, she was going to accept him.

SO THIS WAS what it was like to make love, Amaryllis mused, riding high on a cloud of sex and adrenaline.

The picture in the mirror was a vulgar comparison to such a romantic notion. Her hands were bound high over her head and her legs were spread where she stood on two blocks, making her tall enough for her lover to thrust inside her with ease. Her breasts bounced and tummy jiggled while Lucian stuffed her ass with his thick cock. The burn in her channel, combined with the incessant vibration in her cunt, sent orgasmic waves rippling through her, each one hinting at something larger with the next pass.

Behind her Lucian was all hard planes and steely concentration. Sweat highlighted all of the muscles of his body. His hips ground the vibrator onto her throbbing clit. The act was so beastly, so carnal, yet she'd never felt so loved in her life.

Tears streamed down her face as she let go and gave her pleasure to Lucian. She sagged against him, flowing with his movements, allowing him to drag her from one sensation to the next.

Lucian had been right, he did know what she needed. He knew just how to touch her, how hard and how fast. Every time she moaned or cried out, his satisfaction wrapped around her, driving her to another orgasm, which fed back to him in a never-ending cycle of give and take.

From half-slitted eyes she admired the flex of his body and the strength of his hands as he cupped and kneaded her breasts with his long fingers.

"Amaryllis. Look at us. Look at me," he rumbled in her ear.

Her gaze found his in the mirror. As bright as lightning, the white of his irises flashed with intent. "In the name of the Gods, I claim you as my bonded mate."

The Sacred Vow.

Disbelief froze her in place. Was this really happening? The night before was a blur of pleasure, now there was no mistake. Lucian was staking his claim. No more hiding, no more games. Once the bond solidified, there was no going back.

Did she have the courage to accept?

"In my hands I hold your life and your love. Two precious gifts I ask you to entrust in my care." His voice roughened as his thrusts lost their smooth rhythm and became more frantic. "In return I promise to be all things you need."

His fingers dug into her breasts until it felt as if he actually held her hearts in his hands.

"Say you accept me. Say you accept my gift and bond as one for eternity."

The pressure of his body on her, in her, eased as they fused into one entity. They breathed as one, thought as one. When her muscles clamped down on the two phalluses, she was in his mind, experiencing the delicious squeeze in his loins. The fire gathering in his balls boiled in her belly and their lungs burned with each strangled breath. An electric charge shot down her spine at the same time Lucian released his cum into the tight clench of her ass.

"Amaryllis," he gritted out. "Do you accept me?"

"Lucian," she cried. "Lucian. Yes."

Fireworks exploded into a thousand sparks, buckling her knees and enveloping her body in a white-hot mass that consumed her whole. The roots of her hair turned a raven black that poured down to the tips. Flames tore through her, turned her inside out and remade her into someone new.

On the edge of her consciousness was Lucian. He cradled her in his strong arms as well as his mind. Euphoria edged his concern as he gently released her from the cuffs. And the love, there was so much she was drowning in it. His love was like floating on a velvet cloud, new and sensuous. The power of his devotion rocked her to the marrow of her bones, leaving her unable to do nothing more than cling helplessly at his mile-wide shoulders and sob uncontrollably against his chest.

He set her in the center of the bed then moved to step away. She clutched at his arm. "Don't leave me."

"Never." He kissed her palm. "But I need to care for you."

Thank the Gods for his super speed. He was back within seconds with a wet washcloth and a towel. His touch was reverent as he bathed the sweat, lubricant and cum from her body. A sharp contrast to the way he manhandled her just a few scant moments before, but not any less passionate. Once she was clean, he crawled across the mattress, pulling the covers to her chin and taking her in his arms.

"It's a good thing I can sense your joy," Lucian said with a touch of laughter in his voice. "Otherwise all of these tears would have me worried."

Her chuckle came out in a wet snort. "I apologize. I just never imagined I could feel this way."

"It is quite amazing." He brushed his knuckles down her cheek, following the curve of her jaw and the column of her throat. A lock of blonde hair tangled around his fingers. He rubbed the dry stands against his thumb. "Why is this hair different than the rest?"

Heat blazed across her cheeks and she cleared her throat. "Part of my hair turned black and I bleached it white."

The lines around his mouth deepened. "Ah, Amaryllis. I'm sorry I ever gave you cause to regret our mating. I hope in time you can trust how truly grateful I am to have you in my life."

She reached up and rubbed her fingertip over the frown line between his eyes. "I think I understand you better now, *elskan*. You carry so much burden on your shoulders. I swear I can feel the weight of it myself. Please allow me to ease some of that stress. I want to be your partner, not another obligation."

"You were never an obligation. However, I do sense that it is in your nature to test me." He plumped her breast in his hand, thumbing the nipple to a hard peak. "I guess I'll have to keep you so sated you won't have the energy to cause mischief."

He took the pink tip into his mouth as she heard the front door open and close with a bang.

"Hello," Dhavin called out. "Since I no longer had the urge to fuck everything standing, I figured it was safe to return. I have news to discuss before you two start up again."

Amaryllis shared a smile with her mate before dashing out of the bed and retrieving his shirt from the floor to cover her nakedness. She turned to find him reclining against the pillows with his hands behind his head. The sheet draped low across his hips did nothing to conceal the erection growing beneath the cotton.

She hated to see all that magnificent bronze skin covered up, but Dhavin's footsteps coming up the stairs compelled her to ask. "Will you not dress?"

He shrugged and gave her a grin full of promise and sex. "What's the point? As soon as we're alone I'm going to bury my cock inside you. It will take too long to undress."

With a wicked laugh of her own, she practically floated back to the bed where she bounced onto the mattress and pressed a smacking kiss to his lips.

"Enough of that," Dhavin interrupted. "Thanks to you two, every couple in a half-mile radius is engaging in intercourse right now. I beg you, please tone it down in the future."

"We need to find you a girl, Dhavin," Amaryllis said as she snuggled against Lucian's side.

"Lucian will share. Won't you, Lucy?"

She placed a restraining hand on her husband's chest as he lunged forward with a growl. Dhavin should thank his lucky stars she had the strength to hold her husband back. "He's teasing. Besides, he never made me scream."

Dhavin gave a theatrical gasp. "That's hurtful. But in all

seriousness, congratulations on your bonding. I know that in each other you have found the happiness you both deserve."

"Thank you, cousin."

"As much as I'd love to allow you more time to bask in your bonding, I have news on Bale."

The grim tone in his voice raised the hair on her arms. "What happened?"

"Bale was spotted at your club asking questions. Kristos found him as he was leaving and followed. They came upon some sort of skirmish amongst a felonious tribe. Bale unleashed hell, slaughtering all but two, and engaged Kristos in battle in the process."

"How is Kristos?"

"He's fine. Confirmed that Bale is a tough target to beat, but also discovered that Bale is having difficulty siphoning through the glutton of emotions on this planet. We can use that to our advantage."

"Yes," Amaryllis murmured. The apprehension twisting her stomach tightened. "What else? I sense more."

"You friend, Jorges, was injured."

"What did Bale do to Jorges?"

"Nothing that a couple of stitches couldn't fix."

Bile rose in her throat. "Heaven's light."

"He's all right. The wounds were meant to warn, not kill."

As if that made her friend becoming a target any better. "That's it. We end this now."

She jumped out of bed and retrieved her jeans from the

floor, tugging them on in jerky movements.

Lucian stopped her hand when she reached for the buttons on the shirt. "*Akita*, I don't like how you just shut me out. What are you thinking?"

"I'm done hiding. He was trained by you, Lucian. He will be patient and methodical while waiting us out. Meanwhile my friends will be terrorized or killed while we sit on our asses. Not acceptable. If Bale wants me, he'll have me."

Lucian made a sound that was half laughter, half strangled gurgling. "Let's not be stupid. That's not what I mean," he hastened to add when she arched her brow. "I understand your frustration and I know you hurt for your friend, but you cannot walk up to the man and believe you can have a reasonable conversation. He wants us dead. I will not give him the opportunity to succeed."

"And I cannot stand by and do nothing," she shouted, angry more about the situation than at Lucian. "There are four of us and one of him. We've lived here longer. We know the environment better and are more aware of our abilities. We use them and end this threat. Now. Call Kristos and bring him in." She picked up Lucian's pants and threw them at him. "And put some clothes on. I cannot concentrate when your cock is pointing at me."

"Your Highness," Dhavin interceded and shook his head at the fuming giant behind her. "With all due respect, I ask you to take but a moment to let us think of a plan that does not put any of us in danger, especially a newly mated wife and her husband who looks as if he's two seconds from strapping you to that table and leaving you there forever."

Lucian wouldn't. A glance at him over her shoulder confirmed he'd do just that. "General Lucianllanos. What say you? I will listen to any suggestion you have, however, if I am not satisfied, I will handle this myself. And you better have something stronger than a pair of handcuffs to tie me down."

His eyelashes fluttered and his nostrils flared, yet he restrained the eye roll she knew he was dying to let loose. His chest rose with a deep breath. "Gods grant me the strength for you are glorious when you are riled. Come to me. I need you in my arms for just a moment to remind me what we're fighting for."

And like that, her anger deflated. When he held open his arms, she flew across the room and threw herself against his chest. Yes, ultimately it did not matter how Bale was defeated as long as he was put down quickly. Lucian didn't want her near danger. Understood. She wanted him nowhere near the action as well, but this endless waiting for the other stiletto to drop was driving her insane. No one could live their life on hold forever.

Lucian ran his hand down her hair. "Believe me, *akita*, I share your frustration. There is nothing I want more than to stay here and make love to you and not worry about our safety. I will end this threat against us, and it will happen tonight. I created this Bale. I will end him."

"Not alone." She squeezed him tight. "Bale is looking for

the three of us. He won't make a move unless he knows exactly where we all are, otherwise he'll think it's a trap."

"She has a point."

Lucian shot a scowl at his cousin. "Nonetheless, we will proceed with caution. Actually, Amaryllis, your comment about cuffing you gave me an idea."

"Excuse me—"

He placed a finger over her lips. "Not for you."

However the heat in his eyes suggested it was only a matter of time before she found herself bound and in his control. The lascivious possibilities reawakened her wanton appetite, liquefying her center and raising her body heat twenty degrees.

Dhavin cleared his throat. "Your idea, cousin?"

"Right." He blinked rapidly and took a step back but kept his arm around her shoulders. "There is a mineral in the Earth's soil that has the ability to drain our powers."

That got her attention. "Drain our powers? How?"

"If we're exposed to this element, it starts to deplete our powers within seconds. It leaches our strength and leaves us weak and nauseous."

"Sounds like you've had personal experience," Dhavin noted.

"I have. Kristos discovered the element by accident when he went into a pit to rescue Brett. In its natural form, the effect happens fairly quickly, however when the molybdenite is reformed into a chain, the thickness of the links affects how long it takes to drain us completely."

Her intuition picked up a vibe she didn't like. "How do you know so much about the side effects?"

"I've done some experimenting."

"Some? How much?" A red flush graced his cheeks and his lips tightened. "You wrapped yourself in these chains, didn't you? You drained your powers?"

He nodded.

"What did this mineral do to you? What can it do to us?"

"Prolonged exposure results in flulike symptoms. After about eight hours of exposure you will succumb to the darkness."

"Meaning what?"

"I was unconscious for three days."

"Lucian! You shouldn't have risked your life that way."

"Kristos wasn't going to volunteer, and that exercise gave us powerful knowledge."

"You could have died."

"But I didn't."

"We'll need another," Dhavin interjected. "Someone who can hold on to this chain without draining their powers. Is there anyone we can trust with the knowledge of who we are? What about one of Brett's deputies?"

"My friend, Jorges. If he's up to the task," Amaryllis suggested. "He's my most trusted confidant, and he's already met Bale. He'll understand."

"General?"

"I agree. Since Bale is having difficulty siphoning emotions, let's make sure we project as many of our own as loudly as possible. In the confusion we can hide the presence of Amaryllis' friend."

"That's it then." She clapped her hands together. "We lure Bale to meet us, wrap him in this chain and end him."

"In a rudimentary sense, yes. But it won't be that simple. We must prepare for any possibility."

"Then let's not dally." She stripped off Lucian's shirt and handed it to him before reaching for her own. "We can strategize in the car."

"*We'll* strategize in the car," Lucian corrected. "You will stay out of the way somewhere safe."

She was smart enough to keep her mouth shut. Lucian may think her fragile, but before the night was over, he'd have no doubt she was as willing and able to fight for their future as he.

Chapter Nine

A T FIVE A.M. The Cavern was at its most quiet. The last patron had long gone home, the flashing lights were dark and a yawning silence replaced the pounding bass of dance music. Without the energy of a few hundred bodies engaging in their secret desires, one might think the vast interior would feel cold and vacant, yet the electric hum of heightened adrenaline filled every nook and cranny until the building pulsed like a living, breathing entity.

Amaryllis stood in the darkness under the stairs and ignored the sensation of fire ants crawling over her skin. Lucian was pissed at her and his family and doing a terrible job of controlling his anger. As if she wanted to spend her evening facing down a killer. Her husband's unwillingness to put her in danger was understandable, however not even he could argue with Dhavin's logic and Kristos' support.

She resisted the urge to look up into the catwalk where Jorges waited with thirty pounds of molybdenite chain. Thankfully her friend had been incredibly open-minded about her origins and their current situation when she confided her secret upon their return to the city.

"You're a real princess. From one of Saturn's moons," he

had repeated slowly after she told him her entire story. "And the reason your hair is now black is because you've bound your emotions to this guy." He pointed to Lucian. "The same man you wanted castrated three nights ago."

She grinned as her husband shot her an affronted frown. "Yes."

Jorges had looked at the quartet surrounding him then burst out laughing. He immediately groaned and pressed a hand to the bandage covering the stitches at his side. "Why am I not surprised? Oh this whole bonded-mate thing, yeah, shocked on that front, but you being a royal of a race of aliens, no, not surprised at all."

And that was why she loved Jorges.

Did she hate involving him in such a dangerous scheme? To the point she was ready to vomit, but he was the unknown who might swing the battle in their favor. Even with the odds being three-to-one, they understood the prudence of being prepared for anything.

Kristos strode through the front door of the club with sword in hand. From under his cowl his pale-green eyes flashed with anticipation. "He's coming."

Amaryllis flattened her back against the wall. Just because Bale was coming didn't mean it would be through the front door.

"Good evening, gentlemen," a gravelly voice boomed across the hardwood floor, coming from nowhere and every-where at once. "What a pleasure it is to be in your company again. For this little while anyway. Come on. Let's not be shy. You were the ones to issue such a charming invitation. Step out where I can see you."

"You first," Lucian called out. "Or are you a coward?"

"This from a man who hides behind a woman," came the scorn-filled remark before thick fingers slid around her throat.

Before she could gasp, she was dragged onto the middle of the dance floor. Despite the bruising pressure crushing her airway, she fought, not like a pampered princess but like a street brawler, kicking at his legs and digging her elbows into a solid wall of muscle. She reached behind her and dug her fingernails into the soft tissue of his face. The move freed her from Bale's grip for all of two seconds. He caught her by the back of the shirt, spun her around and hauled her against his chest. Their eyes met and he froze with a soft gasp falling from his lips.

His gaze raced over her hair and face. His eyes glittered so blackly, her frightened reflection stared back at her.

"You're mated," Bale murmured. A crack formed in the barricade he held on his emotions and Amaryllis tasted the sourness of his jealousy. He lifted his hand and ran his fingers through her midnight tresses. The jealousy turned to wonder before his lips twisted into a bittersweet smile.

Amaryllis couldn't breathe, but it wasn't fear that stopped her lungs. The man before her was trapped in another time, in another place he missed so much, his sadness banded around her chest. The fist clutching her shirt slackened and his hand began a gentle massage along her spine. She had no delusions that it was affection for her that gentled his demeanor. Bale was lost in a memory so profound, it brought tears to her eyes.

"Tell me about her," she asked softly.

Fire flickered in his eyes that he quickly banked. The black depths turned empty and soulless. "It's a pity you don't get to enjoy your bonding."

"Why do you want me dead, Bale? What wrong have I caused you to come all this way to kill me?"

"It's not personal, Princess. However, unless you've bonded with a human, it may be now. Where is your mate? Who's the lucky man who gets to watch you die?"

"I'm here." Lucian stepped into the light. "Let her go, Bale. Your fight is with me."

"No," she said. "His fight is with himself. I doubt Hamerkind offered you a fortune to come here. What are you really after, Bale?"

"Your mate owes me. His cowardice cost me everything."

"Or was it yours?"

His hand came up and swung, but she didn't flinch. A soft breeze caressed her cheek as Lucian stopped the open-palm slap mere millimeters from her face. She held Bale's hot gaze and looked right into his soul.

Kristos came up behind Bale while Dhavin rushed from the right. At the sound of their footsteps, Bale roared and traced across the room. He withdrew a pistol from his waistband and fired to his right then his left as the *Llanos* dodged the bullets.

Amaryllis stood steady, fully confident that no harm would come to her at Bale's hands.

The brothers on the other hand were completely fair game. Their images were nothing more than blurs of black and gray as they traced around Bale, who avoided their flying fists with a series of bends and twists.

Lucian charged with his sword raised and a battle cry on his lips. His swing caught the arm of Bale's jacket, tearing the fabric as the sharp tip sliced toward his hand, catching the butt of the gun and knocking it out of Bale's grasp. Kristos attacked from the opposite side, every punch aimed to drive Bale to the spot where Jorges could drop the molybdenite on his head.

Bale leapt into the air, flipping over Dhavin, who approached from the rear, and used him as a shield to block the deft swings from the *Llanos'* swords.

Amaryllis was the eye in the center of the storm. A dead calm that built with each grunt and crack of fist against bone. With the clarity born of her station, she saw each man, not in their physical bodies that grappled head over feet in a mix of finely honed skills and moves born of desperation, but down to their spirit.

Dhavin fought for his princess. When Lucian was kicked back against the bar, Dhavin ensured he stayed between her and danger. He was ready to lay down his life, not because it was his job but because he was her friend.

Kristos battled for his wife and the life they built together.

Lucian also fought for his family and the mate who held his hearts, and the brother he felt deserved more happiness than he.

And Bale...

Bale fought because it was all he had. He fought demons born from the guilt over his past actions.

Four men who all fought for the same reason.

Love.

"Stop!" she shouted in a voice so powerful, the walls quaked.

The *Llanos* froze mid-swing. She took the second of opportunity and raced between them to tackle Bale to the floor.

"Now, Jorges!" She jumped off a dazed Bale moments before he was hit in the chest by a ball of thick-linked chain.

The brothers seized Bale's flailing arms and legs while Dhavin wrapped the chain around his body.

"Brilliant move, Amaryllis," Kristos wheezed, bracing his hands on his knees.

Lucian lifted his sword. The light glinted off the sharp blade. "This ends now."

"No." Amaryllis stepped up to their captive. She tilted her head to the right then to the left as she considered the comatose assassin. "Death is not what he needs."

"Yes it is," Lucian argued.

"No. It isn't. Take him to my room."

"Amaryllis, not more than two minutes ago this man tried to kill you."

"No, he tried to kill you." She held up an imperious hand. "This is The Cavern and all who come to The Cavern get what they need. Take him to my room."

Kristos looked back and forth between them, clearly torn between his commander and his princess. She arched a brow at his hesitation. "Kristosllanos?"

He bowed at the waist. "Your Highness." He bent and lifted a weak Bale in his arms as if he were a small babe.

Lucian stepped before her as she moved to follow. "*Akita*, that male made a threat against the throne. The punishment is death."

"That male is running from his mistakes in the past. He needs compassion, not revenge, Lucian. You of all people should be able to empathize since you're so much alike."

He backed away with wide eyes and his skin paled. "We are nothing alike."

"You both are running from the guilt of events you didn't cause. You have to forgive yourself before you can move forward."

"That's the most ridiculous thing I've ever heard."

Amaryllis turned toward her friend. "Dhavin?"

His chest rose with his indrawn breath. "I'm sorry."

He turned and landed a roundhouse kick to Lucian's chest that sent him soaring into the brick wall. Plaster rained from the ceiling and a crack ran up the concrete wall.

Dhavin retrieved a backup length of chain and secured it around Lucian who stared at them in disbelief.

"Why?"

She stood over him and settled her palm against his cheek. "You're in The Cavern. Within these walls you will always receive what you need."

✦   ✦   ✦

DHAVIN WAS A dead man, and his wife was going to get her ass paddled until it burned hotter than the sun.

The drugging effects of the molybdenite were finally wearing off, little good that did him. His eyes felt full of grit and his limbs ached as if he relocated Mt. Rainier rock by rock. Keeping him on his feet was a thick rope that snaked up each leg and around his torso, continuing up his arms to where he was secured to two floor-to-ceiling beams. The only part of him left exposed was his naked cock, which hung half erect from his pelvis. His vision blurred in and out until he focused on a trio of burning candles set on a low table across the room. A few blinks more brought the rest of the room into view. There were about a hundred candles in different sizes clustered around the space decorated solely for sinful activities. If he thought the cottage was a den of vice, it was vanilla compared to this place.

Rich, red drapes hung in elegant swags from the ceiling, cradling the warm mahogany furnishings in their velvet grasp. The elegant décor softened the harsh line of whips and floggers lining the wall and the bold lines of restraining chairs and Saint Andrew's crosses.

Under different circumstances Lucian might have given free rein to the call of the seductive surroundings and willingly allowed Amaryllis to tie him up however she pleased. Now all he felt was the cold terror of uncertainty as it constricted around his chest tighter than the rope.

What devious plan was his princess conjuring? Clever girl chose his cage well. Once his strength returned, it would be no problem to yank the rope from its moorings, but then he would take the beams with it, bringing the roof down upon their heads. She didn't want him to interfere with Bale's punishment. Understood. But why restrain him in such a fashion?

A deep groan drew his attention to the right and his pulse jumped with the implications.

Naked men displayed spread-eagle appeared to be Amaryllis' preferred choice of decoration, he noted as he spotted Bale. The other man was also suspended at the wrist between two beams, but he knelt on the ground with his knees spread far apart. A thin chain of molybdenite was wrapped around each arm from wrist to shoulder and again down each leg. Unlike Lucian, his cock was bound against his belly by a metal codpiece. A black scarf covered his eyes and his even breathing made it difficult for Lucian to tell if he was unconscious or playing possum. Bale's mind was quiet, but that didn't mean he wasn't plotting a hundred scenarios of escape.

The door opened and both men flinched at the sharp sound. Amaryllis entered. A vision of erotic perfection that made his mouth go dry and his head spin from the blood rushing to his bobbing cock. She wore a white gown in a gossamer fabric so sheer it highlighted her pink nipples. The gown was belted around her waist with a wide satin band that made her waist look tiny and her hips and bust round and sumptuous. With her dark hair and swirling lavender eyes, she was a goddess as she floated to stand before him.

She laid her hand against his cheek and brushed her thumb over his lips.

"What are you up to, my little witch?"

Her smile sent a chill down his spine. "Ensuring our freedom," she whispered and swept away in a cloud of silken gauze.

Without the warmth of her touch, he shivered and snapped his teeth together to keep them from chattering. Each step she took toward Bale made Lucian's hands tighten around the rope and his hearts beat so hard, they felt ready to leap out of his throat. The look she shot over her shoulder warned him not to make a sound or interrupt in any way.

When he opened his mouth, she lifted a finger. With a firm shake of her head she mouthed the word, "No."

He bared his teeth but kept silent.

"Balellanos. How are you feeling?" she asked as she untied the sash covering his eyes.

A bitter taste filled Lucian's mouth. In Bale's weakened state his defenses were compromised. Visually he didn't even blink, yet his disgust at Amaryllis' use of his warrior name repulsed him so greatly, it reached across the room to slap Lucian in the face.

Amaryllis didn't let his silence deter her. She continued to coo in a deep, sultry voice. "Earlier you wouldn't answer my questions. Perhaps you'll be more inclined to answer me now."

She ran her fingers through his thick hair, trailing the backs over his cheek and down his neck. Alternating between the pads of her fingers and the scrape of her nails, she caressed him over his chest and shoulders. The only outward response Bale gave was a slight flare of his nostrils, until she pinched his sensitive nipples between her fingernails.

Both men gasped with the pain as a fissure of fire raced down Lucian's belly to inflame his cock.

Bale seemed to notice Lucian's presence for the first time and tried to block his hatred but didn't even come close. His eyes narrowed and a tic pulsed in his jaw as a million pinpricks scratched across Lucian's skin.

Amaryllis looked back and forth between the two men with an interested arch to her brow. "I see there's no love lost here. Tell me, Bale. Why do you hate Lucian so?"

He drew in a large breath but remained silent. With a slight smile, Amaryllis continued to caress his chest, leaving pink lines on his skin as she dug her nails into his flesh. His abdominal muscles flexed the lower she touched and his breath caught as the tips of her fingers slipped beneath the codpiece.

Lucian gasped as heat erupted around his groin. Amaryllis

was twisting the hair around Bale's cock and the sensation traveled straight to Lucian. The biting pain tapered off, leaving him surprisingly aware of his aching erection and the pressure building in his balls.

"The story I heard is you blame Lucian for the death of your family. Is that true? Tell me your story, Bale."

His breath grew ragged and as harsh as a rusty chainsaw.

"Tell me, Bale."

When he continued to remain silent, she pulled away. His body followed, betraying his eagerness for more of her touch.

"What was your wife like? Was she cold? Unfeeling? A vicious, cruel bitch?"

That broke his silence. "She was perfect," he spat. "Gentle. Kind."

Amaryllis smiled. "Beautiful."

"Yes."

"A good mother."

He closed his eyes and sighed. "Yes."

She resumed running her hands over his chest. "How many of Hamerkind's men ambushed your colony?" She stopped her caress when he didn't answer.

His throat worked as he swallowed. "Fifty-five."

She rewarded him with more touching. "How many left that night?"

"Fifty-five."

"How many are alive now?"

"None."

"You killed them all?"

He nodded.

"Good."

He looked at her sharply and blinked with surprise. "What?"

"If I were your wife, I'd want them all to suffer for what they did to me and our child. And you made them suffer, didn't you, Bale?"

"Every last one."

She swayed as she moved behind him. From the side table Lucian saw her retrieve a whip and uncoil the long length. "And who did you kill after that?"

Lucian tensed, sensing Bale's confusion.

Amaryllis ran the blunt end of the whip down his spine and Lucian felt the pressure along his own vertebrae. "After you killed those soldiers, who was next? Tell me. As your wife, I'd have the right to know."

A thin whistle preceded the crack of leather on flesh. Lucian and Bale arched with a surprised hiss as the burn of the lash raced across their backs.

She flicked the whip a second time, scoring his other shoulder. "Tell me, Bale. Tell your wife who it was."

"No one," he panted. "No one she'd know."

"Then why?" She threw the whip twice more. "Why kill if it wasn't for her? Is that who you thought she was? Bloodthirsty? Cruel? Is that how you remember her? As your wife, I'd demand an answer."

With each question, the whip fell in steady strokes. The scorching heat mellowed into a sizzling simmer that tightened all of his muscles and constricted his chest. Lucian bucked in his restraints as did Bale, whose body swayed in time with his punishment, not to get away from the lash but to seek more of the pain.

"Answer me, husband. Did you think I'd be honored by you spilling innocent blood? By living a life drenched in vengeance? Is this the type of father I'd want for my child?" Bale held back a strangled sob. "You were my husband. As my bonded mate, how could you think I would want this?"

Bale froze and Lucian's hearts stopped with him. His throat closed up as a sense of shame filled his lungs, drowning him with such guilt, his knees buckled.

Amaryllis sucked in a breath as her eyes widened at the concession. "You never bonded," she murmured and laid her hand on his shoulder. "Why?"

The big man shuddered and bowed his head.

"I loved you?" she asked.

"Yes," came the choked reply.

"You loved me?"

He closed his eyes and nodded.

She brushed her lips down his corded neck. "Why didn't we bond?"

His grief ripped through Lucian as he whispered, "I didn't trust you."

"That's not true. You trusted me to care for our home and

our family. But that's not what you mean, is it?" She lifted her gaze and stared at Lucian with those all-seeing lavender eyes that speared right to the heart of the truth that both men harbored. "There's a darkness that lives inside every *Llanos*. It allows you to give your life for your people, to fight for innocents like me. It allows you to do unspeakable acts if needed and drives you to live a life of extremes. That darkness is what you couldn't trust me with. Am I right?"

"You were so pure," Bale muttered, lost in his memories. "You deserved so much better than me."

"But I wanted you anyway, Bale." Amaryllis stepped back. "Your fear that I would regret bonding with you kept us apart."

Lucian fought the tears Bale's remorse brought forth. To bond with another was the most sacred and humbling of experiences. You were laid bare, every fear, every hunger exposed to your mate in an inseparable connection. Bale craved dark hunger, he liked the fight, he liked the bite of the whip and the rake of a woman's nails over the welts. Lucian imagined that in Bale's mind, Natalia had been so delicate and pure, he refused to blacken her in any way. It was the same reaction he had when it came to protecting Amaryllis from his darker nature. Only now was he realizing that his mate was more than capable of handling all of him.

"I couldn't." Bale shuddered. "Couldn't give you what you asked."

"And that's why you kill. I died and you were truly on your

own. Alone with the regret that you somehow failed me."

Crack!

She had moved so quickly, Lucian didn't see her lift her hand until the leather struck Bale's back.

"I ask you again. How does bathing in the blood of others make up for your lack of trust? Hamerkind destroyed us, yet you willingly become his lapdog to inflict the same pain. Make me understand, husband," she shouted and let the whip fly.

"I'm sorry," Bale wept. The chains around his wrists kept him from doubling over. The realization of his acts washed over him and Lucian in an icy waterfall that hurt more than the lashes falling on his back and legs. "I'm sorry."

Soon the room became filled with the primal beat of groans, sobs and the crack of leather. Bale's defenses were shattered and all his emotions were funneling directly to Lucian. That's when he realized that Amaryllis had been right.

Along with the pain came relief and with it, pleasure. Yes, in this he and Bale were very much the same. They both failed their families, yet no one else believed as they did, and so no one gave them the punishment they felt they deserved. Lucian's isolationism, Bale's descent into ruthless killer were attempts to atone for crimes they believed they committed, but it wasn't enough. It would never be enough. Until a penalty was carried out by someone else's hand, the sacrifice would never outweigh the guilt.

Amaryllis was the avenging goddess who understood exactly what they needed. Her pale skin shimmered with perspiration and the skirt of her gown billowed around her. Her lavender eyes glittered with determination and a knowledge that sent a bolt of heat from his chest to his groin.

"Give me your darkness," she commanded them. "Let me take care of you and give you what you need."

Lucian couldn't look away from the tableau before him as sweat poured off him. His cock was so stiff, the slightest breeze coming from the whip was as firm as a lover's grasp.

The buck and sway, the writhing bodies, as Amaryllis worked both men over like a master conductor was breathtaking. Her will was strong, yet Bale continued to hold out, relishing in his punishment but maintaining a thread-thin hold on his emotions.

Amaryllis narrowed her stare and swung her arm in a round arc, the tip of the whip kissed his tight sac, detonating the last of his control.

Lucian clenched his jaw, holding back a scream as his cock erupted and his seed jutted out onto the floor. His head swam as if filled with helium as he drifted in and out of consciousness.

Amaryllis dropped the whip and wiped at the sweat on her brow. She wrapped her arms about Bale's heaving shoulders and found Lucian with her steady gaze.

When she spoke, her words were for her mate as well. "You were meant to be more than a harbinger of death. Your purpose is to fight for justice because no one understands injustice better than you. Not even our great powers can change the past, and wallowing in regret dishonors those who loved us. You have been given the gift of today and the possibility of tomorrow. Don't fix yesterday's regrets by making new ones. Live, truly live. Use your wife's memory to do good. That's how you can honor her."

Lucian, so overwhelmed with love and pride in his wife, collapsed. The ropes around his arms were the only thing keeping him from tumbling to the floor.

A strong arm wrapped around his waist, startling him. Male. Solid. Lucian struggled to focus on the man loosening his bindings. It was the smug grin stretching his lips that revealed his identity.

"Don't be angry with her, cousin," Dhavin said as he helped Lucian down. "She loves you. As do I."

"Which is why I haven't taken you out at the knees," he slurred.

Dhavin half-dragged him to a bed and helped him lie down. Lucian kept an eye on his mate who was releasing Bale from his cuffs. Jorges worked the chain and stepped back as Amaryllis lifted Bale in her arms and set him on a second bed. After Bale was secured to the headboard by cuffs around his wrists, she hurried to Lucian's side.

"Thank you for not being mad at me." She brushed the hair from his damp brow.

He caught her hand and pressed it to his lips. "You would have made a magnificent queen. I am so proud to be your mate."

Her eyes sparkled. "I'll be reminding you you said that later. Please, let Jorges see to you. I need to care for Bale."

"Go to him."

She pressed a kiss to his forehead then fit their mouths perfectly together in a kiss that was more about their bond and respect than about lust.

What Gods had he pleased to receive such a treasure? Lucian sighed and continued the descent from the wild high.

"You're a lucky man, Lucian," Jorges murmured as he bathed the sweat from Lucian's arms.

"That I am." He allowed his eyes to close, but not all the way. He needed to have her in his sights and bask in her loving gaze as she glanced his way. "That I am."

Chapter Ten

AMARYLLIS KEPT ONE eye on her sated husband and the other on the broken warrior shaking violently on the bed. She ran a cool cloth over his body, removing sweat and tears from his golden skin.

Bale and Lucian were made from the same mold. Both sturdy in muscle but incredibly weak when defeated. One-hundred-ten percent of their effort was not enough. Those they loved were sacred and any slight against them was a sign of their failure. They allowed their capacity to love to become their greatest weakness.

Only when they were broken down to their essence could they have the capacity to comprehend that they were part of a whole. They were but a single cog in the wheel of humanity and not solely responsible for the continuation of the universe. Amaryllis imagined that for these two men, a fact of such magnitude would be difficult to accept.

With softly murmured words and tender touches, she eased Bale down from the rush of submitting to his desires and fears. Tonight he took a small step toward the light. An important step, for certain, but he had a long journey back from the darkness he had resided in for so long. His path was still in his hands, but Amaryllis was confident he would continue in the right direction, especially with the support of her and Lucian.

"Why?" Bale whispered. His eyes drifted open to gaze at her with a mixture of awe and humility creasing his brow. "Why?"

"You had a need. It is my duty to see to my people."

He shook his head, as if unable to comprehend such compassion. "Lucian was right. You are a queen worth fighting for."

"Are you swearing your fealty to me, *Llanos*?"

He drew a deep breath before answering. "I am."

Amaryllis let the statement hang in the air like a promise. Bale's devotion wasn't her objective, but it was a gift she'd gladly accept as quietly as it was offered.

A few more seconds passed when he asked, "What's it like? Being bonded."

A giggle burst from her lips. "It's the most wondrous and maddening thing to ever befall a person."

"And it frightens you," he noted with a quiet surprise.

"Yes. Right now I can feel Lucian's love for me, his pride that I am his mate. But I can also taste his worry. Will he be able to provide for me in all ways? Will he have the courage to let me have my independence when all he wants is to lock me in a cage?"

"I doubt a cage will hold you." He shied away from her touch. "You don't need to care for me any longer. I'll be fine.

Go to your mate. I can taste his hunger for you. Go, Your Highness."

She placed a kiss on his forehead. "Rest, my *Llanos* warrior."

She pulled a velvet drape to afford him some privacy then hurried to her husband's side.

"Wait." Lucian stopped her with a raised hand before she reached the bed. "Take off the dress."

The force in his command sent a current of heat through her veins. He propped himself up on one elbow and readjusted the position of his growing erection. The leashed power in his hot gaze and coiled muscles charged the air between them, ratcheting up the temperature as control shifted from her to Lucian.

She slowly pulled her arms out of the filmy sleeves and shimmied the gown down her body. Lucian held out his hand, pulling her onto the bed and into his arms the moment their palms touched.

His kiss was hard and fiery. A final warning that his will would be obeyed and a wicked promise Amaryllis was frantic to collect.

Lucian pulled back and ran the tips of his fingers over her cheek. "I love you. All of you."

A lump formed in her throat as the truth of his words cascaded over her in warmth and softness. She kissed his fingers, too overcome to speak.

"I need, Amaryllis." He pushed at her shoulders, fisting his heavy cock and guiding the wet tip to her lips. "Open that pretty mouth and suck me deep."

Oh yes, her general was in charge. Just how she liked it.

She licked her lips and eagerly took the rigid shaft to the back of her throat. His legs fell open as he held her by the hair, taking his pleasure as he saw fit. That left her hands free to stroke his thighs and hips, leaving pink welts with her nails as she ran them up his legs to his tight sac.

Lucian released a moan of pure bliss then hissed as she scraped his length with the edge of her teeth and her tongue danced along the underside.

"*Ack jus, akita*, you're going to make me come. Up." He pulled at her hair. "I want to hear you scream. On your knees. Ass high in the air."

She obediently climbed to her knees and lowered her chest to the mattress. Her hearts beat so hard, she swore they made the mattress vibrate. The bed dipped as Lucian disappeared from her field of vision. She gasped when his big hands tilted her hips higher. He spread the cheeks of her ass wide and notched the head of his cock at her entrance.

"Please, Lucian."

"You're so wet. You like sucking my cock, don't you?"

"Yes. Gods yes."

He drove deep and fast, lodging all the way to the balls in one lunge.

Amaryllis slapped her hand against the mattress to keep from pitching forward. She braced her knees farther apart to steady herself against Lucian's powerful thrusts. Now it was her turn to fight for breath as he took her hard and fast.

This was not a gentle lovemaking but an all-out carnal assault meant to rob them both of their senses. He ran his hands over her shoulders, down her breasts to tweak her nipples before delving into the folds of her sex to rub her clit.

"That's so good," she groaned and arched her back to take his thrusts deeper.

She lifted her sex-drugged eyelids and was caught by Bale's dark gaze.

The curtain had been brushed aside and Bale watched them with a deceptively blank expression on his handsome face. He might not have looked it, but he was intensely interested in their coupling. The muscles in his arms flexed, the links of the broken cuffs jangling softly. His chest rose in a rapid rhythm until it matched her own ragged breathing. Most of his body was concealed by the drapery, but she was able to see down the line of his torso to the jut of his hard cock.

Curiosity and longing shone in his eyes, not for her specifically, but for a love and connection he had been too afraid to trust in. She hoped he could see the power that came from entrusting one's inner self to another. Was it frightening? Bloodcurdlingly so. But the reward was far greater than the risk.

"You need more, don't you?" Lucian panted in her ear and nipped at her shoulder.

"Yes. Yes," she sobbed.

He smoothed his hands down her spine and cupped her hips. His fingers fanned out over her rear and his thumbs brushed the crease of her ass before he pushed both digits into the tight hole.

"*Jesu*, Lucian!" she screamed as the sharp burn stole the last of her composure. "Don't stop. Please, don't stop."

Stripped to her animalistic core, she pushed back into the double invasion and begged for more of the intoxicating delirium that came with being pushed to the edge. How long could she ride along the precipice? Torn between the high of orgasmic ecstasy and the white-hot cleansing that came with the exquisite rapture.

Could Bale feel her? Could he taste both hers and Lucian's desire? Did he understand that as a bonded mate, you didn't have to hide your darkness, because your mate shared the same hungers?

She reached out with her powers and fed him her frenzied emotions, pumping him with an elixir of sex and love that made his cock bob in the air. She watched the cum drip from the narrow tip and wondered about his flavor, flicking her tongue along her lips as if she could taste him on her tongue.

That was enough to push Bale into oblivion.

The veins in his neck stood out in stark relief as bit his lip and his back arched. His cock erupted, splashing his belly with his cum. His orgasm struck her and Lucian like a concussive wave. Her pussy seized, clamping firmly down on Lucian's shaft so that she felt the kick in his cock as he bathed her walls with his cum. Even after his shout of release stopped ringing in her ears, his hips kept thrusting in an erratic rhythm, drawing out the pleasure until she wept with the onslaught.

Overcome by Lucian's acceptance of her sexuality, she sobbed. Words were only hot air, but actions spoke volumes. To have him in her mind, loving her, all a dream come true. He wrapped her in the safety of his love as strongly as the arms that gathered her close. He swept the hair out of her eyes and fruitlessly wiped at the tears streaming down her cheeks. Kisses were peppered over her face and along her shoulders as soothing palms tried to calm her teeth-chattering shudders.

"I'm—so—so sorry," she stuttered.

"You're perfect and amazing," Lucian murmured into her ear.

She glanced over his shoulder and saw the curtain was once again drawn, but the velvet was no barrier against the well of grief that bled out of the big man who was alone on the other side.

She moved to jump off the bed to ease some of his pain, but Lucian stopped her, pressing his lips to her ear to whisper, "No, *akita*. Not yet. Let him have his space."

"He hurts," she whispered back. Bale's pain made her realize how fortunate she was to have Lucian and how devastating it would be to lose him.

"I know." He pulled her down by his side. "He'll be okay, Amaryllis. You've changed him. I'm so proud of you."

Tears slid down her cheeks. There was so much she wanted to say, so much she wanted to share about how amazing she found her mate, but exhaustion robbed her of speech and she melted into Lucian's arms, convinced she was the most loved woman on Earth.

✦   ✦   ✦

"GOING ANYPLACE IN particular?"

Bale paused with one hand on the door leading out of The Cavern. He turned toward where Lucian stepped from the shadows. He shrugged. "Not a clue."

Lucian nodded and tucked his hands into the pockets of his jeans. "Do you have the means to return to Skandavia?"

"Yes."

While the reply was in the affirmative, Lucian knew Bale would never return to the homeland.

"Here, take these, please." Lucian withdrew a cell phone and some cash from his pocket. "I know you're capable of taking care of yourself, but Amaryllis will be angry if I didn't send you off with something. Don't know how familiar you are with the technology here, but it's a communications device. All of our numbers are programmed in the phone. Please call if you have need. We'll be there."

Bale took the offerings. His brow furrowed as he rubbed his thumb over the screen. With a nod, he placed the items in his jacket pocket. For several long seconds he stared at Lucian. His lips pinched and rolled with the words that showed in his eyes yet remained unsaid. "Good luck to you and your mate,

Lucian."

"Thank you, my brother." He held out his hand, palm up with his fingers curled to form a cup.

More ticks of the clock passed before Bale locked his fingers around Lucian's, completing the yin to his yang. They then grasped each other around the forearm and bowed at the waist.

Bale stepped back and opened the door to late-afternoon sun. He blinked at the bright light, hesitating with his hand on the door. His chest expanded with a deep breath, then he stepped through the exit, the door closing softly in his wake.

Lucian headed up the stairs to where he left his sleeping bride. Along the way he looked around the kingdom Amaryllis had built for herself. At the moment it was nothing but walls and tables. Catwalks and darkened lights. Each night she opened her doors and tapped into the needs of all who crossed her threshold. True to her word, all were welcome. Even hired assassins.

Perhaps *his* hair color should have changed during bonding to match her silver. He had a feeling his dark strands would quickly turn to white with her as his mate.

He crept into her playroom and paused by the bed to strip off his clothes.

"Did he take the money and the phone?" Amaryllis asked without opening her eyes.

"Yes, he did."

He climbed onto the bed and pulled her against his chest.

He kissed her on the forehead. "If you ever do something as foolish as that again, I will paddle your luscious ass and you will not find it pleasurable."

She snuggled deep and he felt her smile against the area above his hearts. "I believe what you mean to say is, 'I'm sorry I doubted you, Amaryllis, and I promise to trust your instinct in the future'."

He snorted so hard, he hurt his sinus cavity. Once he began laughing, he couldn't stop until his belly ached and Amaryllis slapped his arm. "I promise to pause for a few seconds before trying to impose my will upon you and eventually getting my way. That's the best I can do."

"For now," she amended. She threw her leg over his hips and settled her slick pussy over his hardening erection. "Well, General, the threat is over, the damsel is safe. Do you no longer have a purpose?"

He rolled her onto her back and wedged his hips between her thighs. "Oh no. My purpose has expanded to encompass so much more. First, I endeavor to be a good husband to you and make sure you orgasm frequently and well."

"I approve. Continue."

He smiled and dropped kisses along the underside of one plump breast. "I will also spend more time with my family and be a better brother."

"No one has doubted your love for your brother."

"But I can always improve." He laid his cheek on the soft plane of her belly. "But my most important purpose will be to be a good father."

Silence. A long, long silence.

He looked up to see her staring at him with wide eyes.

"You wish for children?"

"Not today, but in the future, yes. I want to build a family with you." When his senses picked up nothing but shock, he began to worry. "Do you not want children of your own?"

"I've never thought much about it." She gestured to the shelves stocked with whips and tethers and a contraption of straps hanging from the ceiling. "My lifestyle doesn't lend itself to raising a child. However," she bit her lip and drew a breath, "I'm not opposed to the idea. I just never saw myself as someone's mother. Do you think I can be a good mother?"

"Surely you're joking. You'd be a fantastic mother. What do think you've been doing for everyone who walks into this club for the last few years? You are a natural caregiver, *akita*." Her hesitant smile broke his heart. "A fiercer mother than you there will never be."

"And if we have a daughter, I pity the young men who come to win her affection." She giggled.

"Men?" Plural? "No, it will not be a problem since we will have sons."

The husky notes of her laugher beckoned him to join. She cupped his cheeks between her palms and gave him a smacking kiss. "We shall see, General. Now, back to your first endeavor. I believe you mentioned something about satisfying orgasms. I command you to eat my pussy."

"As you wish, my princess."

He pushed her legs wider apart and opened the swollen lips of her sex with his thumbs. Drawing her clit into his mouth, he suckled the nub like a decadent candy. He pushed two fingers into her sheath and tucked the tips against the spot that made her cream in his hand.

"Too fast," she panted. "I don't want to come yet."

"I'll make the second one go slower."

"Ooo, you're evil."

Her body went lax in his hold as she dropped all her barriers and released the full brunt of her emotions.

The force punched him in the gut, bending him in two. He was there with her as the pressure tightened in her belly and her hearts felt ready to burst out of her chest. She moaned, he groaned. She trembled, he shook. Her cream flowed like syrup and his balls drew tight to come. He ground his hips against the mattress in a vain attempt to gain some control.

"Lucian." She gripped two fistfuls of sheet and arched with a gasp. "Lucian!"

Her orgasm sparked over his skin like a chain of firecrackers. With herculean strength, he dragged himself to his knees and worked his cock into her dripping channel. His eyes rolled back with pleasure and his cock twitched, but he kept on feeding her his length in slow, measured thrusts.

Her cries quieted into deep, keening moans. The scrape of her fingernails raking down his back made his jaw clench, yet he kept up the relentless pace, loath to end the sensation of riding the razor-thin edge to oblivion.

"Lucian, I'm going to come again." She dug her fingers into his ass. "Please. I'm going to come." She closed her eyes with a grimace.

"Look at me," he commanded.

Her amazing eyes snapped open and she bucked beneath him. Her cunt squeezed his shaft in short, sweet sucks.

His orgasm swept over them both in strong pulls that wrung every drop he produced. He wanted to shout, wanted to tell her how much he loved her, but all he managed was a guttural growl and panting breaths.

"I know, my love." She wrapped him in her soft arms and legs. "I know."

"You've ruined me," he gasped out of his dry throat and collapsed in an ungraceful heap on top of her. "I can't move."

Her breasts shimmied with her rough chuckle. "You can have a moment to rest."

"Good." He closed his eyes, already drifting asleep as she rubbed soothing circles over his back.

"Not too long, love. We have much to decide."

"Hmm-mmm," he murmured with half an ear.

"I'm thinking we should start by deciding where to live. I must check on the restaurant and the club. Then there's the vacation to plan that you promised to take. And of course, we have to find time for my training."

His eyes flew open at that. "Training?"

"Yes. To become a Chameleon."

Surely she jested. Right? *Right?*

Judging by her steady gaze, she wasn't.

"No. Absolutely not."

"I know that you aren't going to give up the armor, and I want in on the action. I have talents. Let me help others."

He stopped her with a quick kiss. He mentally was not prepared to deal with Amaryllis at the moment. "How about we focus on getting through today. Starting with food and more sex."

"For now." Her serene smile sent a flutter of unease rolling in his gut.

Ya, his hair was definitely going to turn gray.

About Anna Alexander

Anna Alexander is the award winning author of the Heroes of Saturn and the Sprawling A Ranch series. With Hugh Jackman's abs and Christopher Reeve's blue eyes as inspiration, she loves spinning tales of superheroes finding love. Anna also loves to give back and has served on the board for the Greater Seattle Romance Writers of America as chapter president and on the committee for the Emerald City Writers Conference.

Sign up to receive news about Anna's latest releases at http://eepurl.com/Q0tsz

Website

annaalexander.net

Facebook

facebook.com/pages/Anna-Alexander/282170065189471

Twitter

https://twitter.com/AnnaWriter

Newsletter

http://eepurl.com/Q0tsz

Also by Anna Alexander

Heroes of Saturn Series

Hero Revealed

Hero Unleashed

Hero Unmasked

Hero Rising

Men of the Sprawling A Ranch Series

The Cowboy Way

The Marlboro Man

To Have Faith

Elite Metal

Bound by Steele

Adamantium's Roar

Elite Ghosts

Thallium's Submission

www.ingramcontent.com/pod-product-compliance
Lightning Source LLC
Chambersburg PA
CBHW050934120626
46552CB00001B/198